A TANGLED WEB

ORLA
KELLY
PUBLISHING

Susan Newman

Orla Kelly Publishing
27 Kilbrody,
Mount Oval,
Rochestown,
Cork,
Ireland

Dedicated to my beautiful grandson,
Luca Newman

CHAPTER 1

He was aptly named, Sergeant Gwen Cassidy reflected, as she stood in front of the full-length mirror in her flat and surveyed her appearance. Hunter by name and hunter by nature. A wry smile spread across her face as she contemplated the propitious timing of her new secondment. The great man's funeral was underway at this very moment and would, no doubt, be the subject of the fevered rantings of broadsheet and tabloid reporters in tomorrow's newspapers. Well, Gwen wasn't going to shed any tears. On the contrary she felt a quiet satisfaction and almost immediately chided herself. It wasn't all his fault. In fact there were times when she held herself solely responsible.

A few months earlier she had emerged from a disastrous relationship and she was still picking up the pieces. She had fallen head-over-heels in love with Hunter, her boss and a married man. Foolishly she had believed his promises. He had felt exactly the same about her and was definitely going to leave his family and settle down with Gwen.

Looking back she blamed her relative youth for her naivety and her complete lack of worldly experience. A 'green horn', her mother would have diagnosed.

When she had become pregnant she was ecstatic and terrified in equal measure. She would have no problem telling her lover. Perhaps this was the impetus which was needed to progress their plans. So everything would be fine there. It was the prospect of telling her parents which gave her sleepless nights. Staunch Catholics, from a rural Co. Roscommon village, they were both pillars of the community and had taken great pride in their daughter when she had joined the Garda Siochana. She had broken new ground, a pioneer, her father had proudly proclaimed and he had recently developed the habit of saluting her whenever she came home. A little joke, he said,

But, as it transpired, she didn't need to have any fears about telling her parents. The lover's reaction was a revelation. He had now changed his mind, he couldn't possibly leave his family and he didn't think it would be a good idea to continue their affair.

Two days later Gwen was summoned before the 'Top Brass' and informed that low standards and loose morals could not be tolerated within the force. They had been informed by a 'very reliable and respected source' that she was a 'temptress' and seemed to target married men in high positions. They weren't suggesting for a moment that blackmail might have been a motivating factor in her selection of 'partner'. But it wasn't unknown for 'desperate women' to resort to such nefarious actions.

So they had decided to temporarily terminate her contract until she had resolved her 'little problem.' Of course she would be later re-instated on condition that she never divulged the identity of 'the poor man' she had 'led astray.'

Two months later the 'poor man' had been promoted to Superintendent and a week after that Gwen miscarried.

The 'top brass' would call it a blessing for all concerned but Gwen was devastated. She had long since relinquished any hope of trying to rekindle the relationship. In fact the very thought of it turned her stomach but, in truth, most of her anger was directed against herself. No doubt Frankie Byrne, the agony aunt on the radio, would remind her of the thousands of women who had been similarly duped. But that was no consolation.

In the immediate aftermath all her thoughts had been focussed on her unborn child and her determination, in spite of her situation, to give it the best start possible in life.

She was five months pregnant when she was rushed to the A&E in The Coombe maternity hospital. The awful news that the baby was dead was delivered in cold, clinical terms motivated, no doubt, by the line on her Admission's form which read, 'father unknown'.

She had spent the next few weeks recovering in a social wilderness. Eventually she felt strong enough and certainly poor enough to approach her superiors and request re-instatement. After 'careful consideration and Christian reflection' they relented but she would no longer be a uniformed member of the force. She was now in admin where she was seconded to Detective Inspector Thornhill, a native New Yorker hewed on the underbelly of the Bronx and seconded to the Garda Headquarters in Dublin where 'her expertise would enhance and progress', - curtesy of a missive from the relevant Government Department – 'the antiquated practices' within said headquarters. Nobody demurred and she was given enormous latitude within the organisation. She was also the niece of the Minister for Justice.

Gwen's time spent working with Detective Inspector Thornhill was the happiest of her time in the force and her good fortune continued when, suddenly 'some of the Cork crowd had gone rogue and would have to be reined in.' Thornhill was deemed to be the Saviour and was now going to the provinces. Thankfully she insisted that Garda Cassidy would accompany her and, furthermore would have to be promoted to Sergeant. Head Office was catapulted into a maelstrom of indignation and rage but nobody was willing to take issue with Thornhill. So Gwen was summoned before her superiors and informed, through gritted teeth, that she was now a sergeant, against their better judgement. Suddenly and unexpectedly, Gwen was back in uniform and sporting the stripes of sergeant. A transfer to the station in Union Quay in Cork was no hardship for her as her mother's people were from Cork and she had spent many summers on the beach in Youghal when the days had seemed endless and were always warm and there wasn't a dark cloud on the horizon. Perhaps she would retrace her innocent footsteps and re-visit her old haunts. Would it still have that magic, that balm to restore a crushed and broken spirit or was it all just her fanciful imagination?

And here she was, about to embark on her first day in her new base, determined to leave the past behind and re-build her life. She would not allow the shame she had felt to impinge on her new life; rather she would compartmentalise, seal it away in a dark recess in her mind and never re-visit it. Nobody need ever know; however, she had long suspected that Thornhill knew, though she had never broached the subject with Gwen. Now as her reflection stared back at her there was no indication of the darkness which had settled within. Swiftly, she picked up her hat and gloves and left her rather cramped bed-sit. In time she would look for more suitable accommodation but for the moment this would suffice and it had the advantage of its relative proximity to her new station.

CHAPTER 2

The funeral cortege was quite the spectacle as it wended its way to Glasnevin Cemetery. Hundreds of locals turned out to view it. As many Gardai as the force could muster were ordered to walk behind the coffin which was bedecked with the most magnificent wreaths.

Superintendent Alderton, who was in the vanguard of the procession and, proudly representing the Cork contingent, later compared the atmosphere and sense of awe to the moon landings.

Superintendent Geoffrey Hunter, whose remains were now en-route to the nearest cemetery, was universally disliked amongst the police force but prestige and influence trumped any such negativity. So, the uniforms were donned, medals polished until they dazzled and a solemn demeanour exhibited by the top brass for the benefit of the reporters and in anticipation of the widespread Press coverage the following day.

And of course there was the tragic dimension of the whole sorry saga. Two days of sailing around Kinsale harbour with a few buddies, going on well into the night, had culminated in the sudden disappearance, overboard, of the hapless skipper and host. The story that unfolded recalled how, to a man, his fellow sailors had dashed to the rails and shouted ardent cries of encouragement to Hunter as he floundered and writhed before plunging to the depths of the briny waters off the south coast.

A rescue team had been dispatched the following morning to the area where Hunter had last been sighted, not helped by the fact that the eyewitness accounts of where he had disappeared varied greatly, anywhere from the Old Head of Kinsale to 'somewhere' around Hook Lighthouse near Wexford.

And, as was his wont during his lifetime, Hunter resurfaced, unexpectedly, upstream from Kinsale Harbour. Many had marvelled, some unkindly, at how his body had managed to stay afloat for a full three days before berthing on the stony outcrop of Sandycove Island, like a beached whale.

But now, at least, he was being given a dignified send-off and before long a suitably gigantic headstone would be erected, financed from the coffers of the Garda Siochana, courtesy of funds purloined from the wages of the foot soldiers and, no doubt, a serious cut-back in resources.

And thus began a suitable period of mourning for the dear departed and an unholy scramble from within to replace the great man.

CHAPTER 3

The following day, back in Cork again, Superintendent Alderton was in a quandary.

Three months before the terrible event his wife of thirty years had left him, in search of 'some semblance of happiness, always supposing that I can recognise such an emotion after being tethered to a most odious man.' Alderton had helped her to pack and now, suddenly, a telegram had arrived announcing that she was homeward bound. There was every chance, in view of the inevitable reshuffling which would take place at Head Quarters, that her husband might possibly be elevated to the position of Superintendent in H.Q. and such a role demanded a spouse by his side, a First Lady so to speak, in order to host and charm the dignitaries and to curb her husband's more 'unsavoury activities'. Alderton, by no means a humble man, was, nevertheless, fairly certain that such a promotion would not be conferred on him. But why not Deputy Commissioner? That had a nice ring to it.

His musings were interrupted by the trill of the phone. It was Linehan, a fellow Superintendent, holed up somewhere in Leitrim and obviously eager to move to the big city as well. After the usual pleasantries about the awful tragedy, Linehan had quickly moved on to the low opinion which Hunter had harboured towards Alderton and he assumed that Alderton would never be foolish enough to entertain notions of succeeding the late Superintendent with a move to H.Q.

Linehan was a low-life. Alderton was tempted to tell him that his ambitions now exceeded that of Superintendent but, instead, he just slapped the phone down. All this undignified scrambling to replace Hunter was a worrying trend. He was on his third whiskey when the call came. The Chief Commissioner's secretary was passing on the message that Superintendent Alderton was to make himself available to meet Deputy Commissioner O' Toole on a matter of extreme delicacy and urgency at the latter's offices in Dublin, on Monday. Alderton almost genuflected as he eased the phone back on its holder and could feel a huge grin spread across his features. 'Up your's, Linehan,' he muttered as he skipped upstairs to don his uniform before heading into his office.

As the station in Union Quay loomed into view Alderton reflected that this might be his last journey to this establishment as Superintendent. He decided that he wouldn't converse with any of his underlings - no point in risking a deflation of his current bonhomie. But as soon as he entered he realised that there was only a skeleton staff as the three-day mourning curfew was still in place and there didn't seem to be anybody about except the desk sergeant, Moloney, and he didn't count.

The place felt deserted – no demands, no hysteria or whinging - and Alderton decided there and then that when he was promoted he would immediately curtail any further recruitment here in Cork, thereby saving money and enhancing his own promotion prospects even further. Chief Commissioner, perhaps? Well, why not. He could suggest that 'his' station be used as a template on how to run a police force with a skeleton staff and the minimum wage.

He had read recently of some precinct in the States where they had just two police officers, armed, and an intelligent dog. The only dilemma really was who in this place could be trusted with a gun.

He spent the next hour tidying his desk and general surroundings, amazed at the lack of clutter and paperwork. Of course he had long since developed the habit of binning every scrap of paper which had crossed his desk, after the most cursory scrutiny. And now he was reaping the benefits of his rigorous filing system.

In his new position he vowed that he would have a secretary, handpicked by himself, who would be a delight to behold and a soothing presence in the midst of the inevitable mayhem which his Detective Inspector Morecamb seemed to inflame at every hands turn. Anybody over thirty would be immediately excluded and dispatched and then............The phone again! Well, he would just have to get used to all these demands.

"Pick me up from the train station, please. I'm hungry and tired and I've been lugging these suitcases half way across the country. And if you weren't such a selfish husband......."

CHAPTER 4

The weekend was torturous. Margie insisted on a joint effort in order to prepare for her 'current' husband's interview on Monday. An extensive search was made of the house to locate the manuals and documents, 'which any self-respecting eejit would have known to file away'. Alderton decided against telling her about his very efficient filing system in the office and spent Saturday morning 'in search' of all things official which, to his certain knowledge, had long since gone up in smoke. By lunch-time the search was called off and Margie decided to compile her own questions, all one hundred of them, and put her husband through a rigorous exam. A 'dummy-run' she insisted on calling it.

The endeavour was a spectacular failure and by dinner-time they weren't on speaking terms and were occupying different floors in their semi-detached house. Alderton was holed up in the spare bedroom where, thankfully, he had a stash of whiskey. His wife was once again threatening to pack her bags.

Sunday threatened more of the same but it suddenly dawned on Margie that the greatest threat to her husband's advancement was the danger that he might answer truthfully any questions put to him. So she encouraged him to lie to his heart's content. A much more satisfactory arrangement as Alderton had spent most of his adult life in a twilight zone with only the occasional foray into the land of reality and truth.

Margie sat back and marvelled at the ease with which he could tell the most abominable lies, in a most convincing manner and she wondered about the true state of their marriage over the past three decades. It didn't bear thinking about. Still, the prize would be worth it. By the end of her husband's bombastic and truly sensational narrative she was beginning to see her husband in a whole new light, no mean feat considering the spectacles she had witnessed over the years.

Travelling to Dublin at all hours on Monday morning, on public transport, had set their teeth on edge and by the time they reached Heuston Station they were snarling at each other. But later, as their taxi snaked its way through the buzzing metropolis Margie became animated, in a positive way, as she memorised the locations of the famous and expensive ladies' department stores and fidgeted restlessly in anticipation. Alderton kept his eye on the taxi meter and marvelled at the speed with which the numbers clocked up.

Margie's sense of euphoria didn't evaporate as they stepped out of the taxi. Hurriedly she straightened her husband's tie, brushed some fluff from his lapels and gave him a quick peck on the cheek. Her husband staggered back in astonishment and hoped this wasn't a portent of things to come. Later he would blame this trauma for some of the extraordinary events which awaited him behind the mahogany door of the top brass. And all the while the taxi- driver, with his hand stuck out through the window, waited for his tip.

*****

It all started off very well, actually. As soon as he was ushered into the palatial office and sat down opposite three chests of medals he was offered coffee and sandwiches.

The meeting was swift and brutal. Superintendent Hunter's unexplained death would have to be investigated and, as it had occurred down in Cork, it would have to be handled down there. All those on board the yacht were suspects, 'including your good self'.

"Especially you", one of them muttered though Alderton couldn't be sure of the source as he focussed on the enormity of what was being communicated.

Yes, they heard that he had been violently ill.........sea-sickness..... no excuse! The behaviour of all those on board was reckless and irresponsible and cast the entire police force in a very bad light. Shameful, in fact. So, for the duration of the investigation Alderton was to step aside and confine himself to the Cold Cases' Unit and for the foreseeable he was now a lowly Sergeant. His replacement, Detective Inspector Thornhill, now Superintendent, had a proven track record. They didn't mention that they were glad to see the back of her. They would never adapt to the presence of a woman in such a high-profile position and they didn't see why they should. There had also been the worrying realisation that Hunter had been showing an unhealthy interest in Thornhill though that had now resolved itself, thankfully.

For good measure they had added that the highly respected Detective Inspector Morecamb would be the Senior Investigating Officer on the case.

And, as Alderton was digesting that final bit of unsavoury information the awful reality of his situation got even worse. He was being replaced by a woman!

On the journey home the poorly-paid train conductor insisted that Margie and Alderton should sit in separate carriages and then he had to apologise profusely to the other passengers for the horrendous scene they had just witnessed. Sweating profusely he repaired to his tiny office and compiled a long letter of complaint about the calibre of passengers he was expected to allow to board his train, citing stress and the torrent of abuse to which he had just been subjected, 'as laid out below'. A pay rise was the very least he expected and so, by the following day, he had joined the ranks of the unemployed.

CHAPTER 5

It was a city of extremes, Morecamb mused. New York had it all. The glitz, glamour and blatant consumerism cheek by jowl with the strays and waifs and those beaten down by life. Buskers on the streets singing of heartache vying with the saccharine love songs pedalled through shop tannoys. Plates piled high in fast food joints and, a few short steps away, the beggars and the homeless haunt the pedestrians who dare to look at them.

The 'beautiful' people, drawn like moths to the glitter of salubrious hotels, while, further along the street, in the dark and lonely alleyways the destitute seek reprieve in the dregs of an abandoned beer bottle and the lucky ones tap the syringe, feverishly find a vein and taste heaven, if only for a few minutes.

As holidays went, it hadn't been too bad. Their hotel had been satisfactory, the food less so and the beer bloody awful. But Jane had seemed happy. She loved the sheer magnitude of New York, the bustle and noise, the frenetic energy of the place, where nothing was too much trouble in the eateries and assistants were 'missing you already' before you left the premises.

But, homeward bound, JFK airport was a nightmare. Several times they had lost each other until eventually Jane had said he was doing it deliberately. Things didn't improve when Jane was accused of attempting to smuggle two handbags through Security. She tried to persuade them, and everybody in the vicinity, that she'd had the bags on her way over to New York but the tags still attached had weakened her case considerably.

The words 'thief' and 'stolen property' and all sorts of nasty accusations were bandied back and forth until Jane assured them that she had receipts for the items, thereby scuppering her assertion that she had brought them from Ireland. 'Liar' was added to the list of attributes and Jane, in a desperate attempt to salvage her reputation and find 'the bloody' receipts,' had emptied the entire contents of her luggage but failed to locate them.

Morecamb could have told her that she had binned them that morning before they had left the hotel with the express intention of trying to hoodwink the officials but he didn't remind her of that. He had decided to stay out of it when things had kicked off, knowing that should he intervene, he would fall foul of both sides. So, he kept a safe distance and tried to conjure up an image of his first frothy pint of Guinness, after an absence of two weeks. American beer had been a very poor substitute.

Eventually an impasse of sorts was reached. Jane's luggage was now considerably lighter....two bottles of perfume and three pairs of denim jeans had also been located in the search for the receipts....... and the Airport Police had reined in the sniffer dogs and left.

Once on board the aircraft they became separated again but neither of them complained. As they had mounted the steps Jane had berated him for his cowardice. Any decent, self-respecting boyfriend would have stood up for his girlfriend and the least he could have done was threaten them with arrest. What was the point in being a Detective Inspector if all he could do was stand there with his hands idly by his side. When he had pointed out to her that American cops were armed she had told him he was just making excuses.

So, the mix-up in the seating allocation, which 'is your fault, Jim' proved a god-send and each headed to opposite ends of the plane.

Morecamb slept fitfully for most of the flight and it was a huge relief when they negotiated passport control in Shannon Airport without incident. Morecamb was glad that they had booked into a Limerick hotel for the night because, in spite of his trans-Atlantic snooze, he still felt groggy and he started to imagine his first pint before falling into bed.

"Detective Inspector Morecamb?" asked a burly individual who was approaching them as they emerged into the daylight. "Detective Sheehan, sir. I've been instructed to bring you straight to the station in Cork, sir. And Madam, of course."

Morecamb didn't look at 'Madam' and sank gratefully into the passenger seat of the squad car. He hadn't been relishing the idea of phoning for a taxi and then waiting around all afternoon for the driver who *"will be with you in ten minutes, sir."*

"So, what's all this about, Sheehan?" enquired Morecamb when they were all settled.

"I don't want to know," snapped 'Madam' from the back seat. "Just drop me off at the George hotel, please."

An uneasy silence settled in the car and Sheehan heaved a sigh of relief as they drew up outside the hotel. Morecamb dragged himself out to help Jane with her suitcase but was told that she didn't need any assistance, thank you very much and he could just clear off.

"Right, Sheehan, fill me in," Morecamb said as he re-fastened his seat belt. "What's all the urgency about?"

Sheehan took a minute to re-join the line of traffic and then announced that he had no idea.

"I'm just following orders, sir, but if you ask me……..."

"Well, I just did, didn't I? Never mind. Wake me when I arrive." And Morecamb settled back into his seat and snored his way to Cork.

Sheehan had heard about Morecamb, of course. An imposing man at 6'4" who seemed to have no bother attracting women. His jet black hair was beginning to recede a little, Sheehan was pleased to see and, even in repose, there was a steeliness to his face. A surly bugger at the best of times apparently but some said he had mellowed since he'd met the new woman. Sheehan couldn't see much evidence of it. He'd been married before of course, according to the rumour machine. Fiona something or other but apparently she was flighty and had buggered off with some low-life. So, for all his film-star looks he still couldn't hold onto his wife. His ruminations were rudely interrupted by the appearance of a tractor in the middle of the road which showed no sign of slowing down.

CHAPTER 6

"It's the end of civilisation as we know it," Murphy intoned quietly as he stared off into the distance.

They were seated in the station's canteen and Morecamb's sergeant of many years was regaling him with the seismic changes which had occurred during his absence. But the only salient point which had registered with Morecamb was the fact that Alderton had been relieved of his duties. Murphy wasn't sure of the details but for some reason he seemed to be quite upset by the turn of events. And his angst seemed to be focussed on Alderton's replacement. 'A woman', Murphy had squealed, as his sweat glands went into overdrive and he complained that there would be no respite now, no difference between home and work.

Before Alderton could offer any words of consolation he was summoned to his new boss's office.

It was such a surreal experience to see a woman in Alderton's seat but a pleasant one.

Morecamb was immediately struck by her relative youth; mid-forties, he reckoned and when she stood to shake his hand he couldn't help but notice a stunning figure. She was almost as tall as he was with shoulder-length auburn hair, striking blue eyes and a smile that didn't quite reach those eyes. A woman not to be trifled with, he reckoned but still a vast improvement on the previous incumbent.

"I'm Superintendent Thornhill," she said and he suddenly realised that she was American. Of course Murphy had omitted to include that nugget of information in the midst of all his twitterings. Time to break the ice.

"Actually I'm just back from the States," he began. "Spent two weeks in New York. Great city and I couldn't get over……" His voice trailed off as he noticed her starting to sift through the papers on her desk.

"Ah, here we are," she interrupted. "Take a seat. Now, your service record, I've been informed, is quite impressive though my predecessor wasn't quite so complimentary. 'A bit of a maverick' was one of his kinder expressions. But I see you have a good level of successful convictions. So, you'll do."

Really! Had he heard correctly? God, what were they landed with?

"That manilla folder there on my desk has all the details of the latest case. Some shenanigans down in Kinsale where our so-called betters decided they would test their limited sailing capabilities to the utmost, resulting in the drowning of one of their number. I'm surprised there weren't more but there you go. Have a look through it and I'll call a meeting in two hours. Close the door after you."

Wow! Morecamb reeled out of the office and headed towards his own. Had they gone from the frying pan to the fire? This was a new departure. You just get used to the incompetence and stupidity of one boss and then you're catapulted into the next realm of surrealism.

In a daze he opened the folder and spent the next two hours poring over reams of notes, witness statements, the ramblings of the top brass who didn't seem to have a clue about events and, of course, the most incoherent statement of them all, Alderton's.

He sat back and laced his hands behind his head. Actually he was quite looking forward to this assignment. Of course, ostensibly, it looked like a straightforward accident but, nevertheless, he was going to milk this one and enjoy himself in the process. He had almost finished compiling notes on his reading when the desk sergeant poked his head around the door and announced that the meeting was about to start.

*****

Morecamb counted about six or seven officers in attendance when he went into the meeting. Thornhill beckoned him to the front of the room where a large whiteboard had been erected. Pinned up on it were the main players in the drama, Alderton's mug shot the most menacing of all. All of the photos were pinned to the board with a dart through the forehead of each. There seemed to be four in all, including the victim. He felt the dart was a nice touch.

Thornhill welcomed all of them and told them Morecamb was the Senior Investigating Officer on the case. She went on to explain that the whole investigation had to be very hush-hush and the top brass had insisted on delicacy and discretion. However, the priority was to establish if it was a drunken accident or if it was a case where one of the jolly sailors had finally snapped and 'did for' the host. She certainly didn't pull any punches.

"So, we'll re-convene in the morning and you can take us through your strategy, Morecamb. Sergeant McClean and Detective Nagle are on your team and a new member is joining us tomorrow. If you need any re-enforcements let me know. Personally, having spent 20 years in the Bronx I'm all in favour of guns so I'll make enquiries on the possibility of firearms. Always a handy tool if you have difficulty beating a confession out of a suspect. Just joking! Anyway, off you go. Sergeant Murphy, will you wait back?"

Before leaving the station Morecamb tried to ring Jane but she had left instructions with the hotel receptionist that she wasn't to be disturbed. Then he borrowed one of the pool cars and, barely able to keep his eyes open, blindly negotiated his way home.

In sheer exhaustion he felt unable to climb the stairs so he threw himself on the sofa and fell fast asleep. The following morning, still exhausted, he washed and changed and decided he would head into the office early. When he glanced at his watch he was horrified to see that it was only 5.30 a.m. He hadn't experienced it before but he presumed that this was jet-lag. He made himself a strong, black coffee before facing the day. The coffee was a habit he'd picked up in the States, a case of 'needs must' as their tea-making abilities were appalling.

Just as he was preparing to leave he noticed that a note, marked 'urgent' had been pushed under the front door. Straight away he recognised the penmanship of Murphy. He had obviously called round the night before. Morecamb vaguely recalled the Superintendent asking Murphy to stay behind after that meeting.

The note was brief and to the point. It simply said, 'I need help.'

CHAPTER 7

When Morecamb entered the Incident Room there was no sign of Thornhill or the extra recruit she had promised. The youthful, effervescent Sergeant McClean was cocked up at the front. Morecamb had worked with him on a previous case and expected the usual level of annoyance. Placed neatly in front of him and with utter precision was an array of coloured pens and an enormous jotter. He would be sorely disappointed, Morecamb felt, if Hunter's death proved to be an unfortunate accident. Beside him sat Detective Nagle. He was new to Union Quay, having previously graced the station in Portlaoise.

He was a man in his early forties, Morecamb guessed, and almost as tall as himself. Certainly well over six foot. McClean looked like a dweeb beside him. Nagle's once black hair was now almost completely grey and when Morecamb shook hands with him his grip was vice-like. A thorn in the side of his superiors, Morecamb had heard, and a man who had no time for the politics within the force and didn't waste any time informing his superiors of his opinions. But he was a shrewd detective. When he put in for a transfer to Cork – his wife was anxious to get back to her family – there was a mixed reaction. On the one hand the bosses were delighted but even they had to acknowledge that Nagle's abilities would be sorely missed.

As the Inspector shuffled his papers into some semblance of order the door swung open and Thornhill entered followed by, presumably, the new recruit. He was surprised to see a woman as the force, whilst not discriminatory in an explicit way, seemed reluctant to enlist women and, when it did, they were usually confined to administrative duties. Thornhill was the exception.

"Sergeant Gwen Cassidy, everyone. Gwen, this is Detective Inspector Morecamb the S. I. O. The other two are Sergeant McClean and Detective Nagle. Carry on, Morecamb."

"Right, welcome, Sergeant Cassidy. I'll just call you Gwen, if that's okay. So, our victim is Superintendent Geoffrey Hunter, age 42. Based on the scant information which we have so far, on August 12th himself and three others set sail from Kinsale harbour with a crate load of alcohol. Calm conditions and everything was splendid for the first day. Primarily because they don't seem to have cast off even though some of them thought they might be half way to Holyhead as the sun went down.

On the following day, according to Alderton's statement, they were joined by another man, a Mr Malachy Cuthbert, an English businessman. But, strangely, nobody else has mentioned his presence, except Alderton. So we need to sort out that little anomaly.

Now, judging from a number of reliable sources we believe that the majority of those on board weren't 'sea-worthy'. Their progress was described as rather chaotic, as if manned by a drunken chicken. Surprisingly, it actually wasn't Alderton in the cockpit. Any questions so far?"

McClean's hand shot up. "Is there any specific reason for believing that a murder was committed? I mean all of those on board appear to be upstanding gentlemen."

"And did you know them personally, McClean?" scowled Thornhill.

McClean immediately returned his attention to his jotter and finished drawing a precise line with the aid of a ruler. He was now on his third page and giving the green biro an outing. Nagle was lounging back in his chair, hands resting lightly on an expansive stomach and every so often he cast an incredulous sideways glance at his neighbour. Gwen Cassidy's gaze never wavered from the incident board, Morecamb noticed, but he knew she was hanging on his every word.

"To answer your question, McClean, we simply don't know but we have to keep an open mind and investigate it thoroughly. Now, moving on, things become rather blurred during the evening of the 14th. The only one who seems certain of his whereabouts when Hunter hit the water is Alderton. He had wobbled off to his bunk in the throes of sea-sickness and was oblivious to the excitement unfolding on deck. Anyway, so we've been told, one minute they seemed to be having a civilised dinner, naturally I use the term loosely, and the next it was panic stations. Hunter, in a rare moment of altruism, thought he saw a body in the water, went over to investigate, leaned over the rails to get a better view in the pitch darkness and simply disappeared.

And in spite of their best efforts," Morecamb continued, "which seemed to comprise solely of shouts of encouragement to the drowning man, it was all to no avail. Any questions?"

"Were there no life jackets on board?" McClean asked, with his pen poised.

"I believe they were ditched in order to make room for the alcohol," Morecamb answered. "Apart from Hunter and Alderton the other stalwarts on board were Superintendent Wallace and Inspector Lonergan. Hunter, Wallace and Lonergan had all worked together in the Serious Crime Division".

"I presume they all gave statements, sir? Apart from Superintendent Hunter, of course."

"Yes, and this is where it gets interesting. Even allowing for the various states of inebriation there is an uncanny resemblance in their accounts. Except Alderton's of course who had his head stuck in a bucket emptying the contents of his stomach and who wasn't discovered until the following morning when the Forensic team went on board. Apparently it was forty eight hours before he could summon the strength to talk, which is a record in itself. Wish I'd been there."

"So, plan of action, Morecamb?" asked Thornhill.

"Well, we need to go through their statements with each of them and we need to touch base with the forensic guys about their search of the yacht to see if they turned up anything suspicious. McClean and Nagle, will you do that? Gwen and I will talk to the widow this afternoon.

Luckily, when I contacted her she told me that she would be in Cork today as she's travelling abroad for a few days due to, and I quote, 'all the emotional stress'. She can spare us an hour, I'm told, before she has to go to the airport. I gathered that her own emotional state takes precedence over the death of her husband. But at least there were no children so she can indulge herself to her heart's content."

No children? Hunter had certainly given Gwen the impression that there were children. What was it he'd said? Oh, yes, he couldn't possibly leave his family. Had she misheard or had she misinterpreted?

The rest of the meeting was a blur for her as she felt the blood drain from her face. She prayed that none of the others had noticed and she was only dimly aware that the Inspector had chosen her to speak to Hunter's widow.

*****

Morecamb caught up with Gwen as she hurried towards the toilet after the meeting.

"Gwen," he called, "I want you to find out what you can about Hunter, before we meet his widow. Maybe a few discreet phone calls to one or two of his former colleagues. Ask the Superintendent if she can give you a few names. I'll be in my office."

As soon as he opened his door Morecamb immediately regretted it. The room was in darkness and when he flicked on the light he spotted the hunched form of Sergeant Murphy sitting over in the corner. His eyes were two black pouches, there were several days' stubble on his chin and he seemed to have acquired a tremor in his hands.

"Have you been drinking, Murphy?" he asked as he went over to the window and snapped open the blinds.

"I left you a note," Murphy rasped, "an urgent one but you didn't bother to come near me this morning in my hour of need."

"Well I'm here now, so, spit it out. Hold on, let me sit down first. Is this going to take long? I have an investigation, you know."

And the floodgates opened.

Even in Murphy's worst nightmares, which are a nightly occurrence by the way, he could never have imagined the misery which had now befallen him. And it was all Morecamb's fault because if he hadn't selfishly taken himself off to the States none of this would have happened.

"You're not making any sense, Murphy, and where did you get that naggin of whiskey? Put it back in your pocket, for God's sake!"

No, he wouldn't be doing that and he finished the bottle with one swig. Yes, he continued, because of Morecamb's actions Murphy had been seconded to the Cold Cases' department to work alongside Alderton and it was only a matter of time before they came to blows.

With the skill of a magician a second naggin was produced from the other pocket.

He had been given a long list of tasks by Alderton including, tea-making duties and collecting his dry-cleaners, he had to sit with his face to the wall, only in extreme cases was he to make eye contact and Alderton couldn't envisage any occasion at all which would necessitate Murphy to utter the spoken word.

"And now I want to know what you're going to do about it, boss."

"I have an idea, Murphy, and I want you to listen carefully." Morecamb went on to outline the Hunter case and Alderton's peripheral role in it.

"So, what I want you to do is to keep your ears open. Make a note of all his telephone conversations and if you get a chance try to draw him out on the sailing trip….."

"I'm not allowed to talk!" squawked Murphy.

"You don't have to. Let him do all the talking. It's what he specialises in."

"So, in other words you want me to spy on him", said Murphy, beginning to sit up a little straighter.

"That's exactly what I need you to do. And I want you to give me a daily update. So, in a way you'll be involved in my case and I'll have a word with the Super and she can slap Alderton back in his box. What do you think?"

"So, effectively I'll be Alderton's equal. Can I tell the wife that I'm now a deputy Superintendent elect?"

"No."

CHAPTER 8

Superintendent Thornhill dashed to her window when she heard the squeal of brakes and the ear-shattering sirens. Looking out she recognised one of their own pool cars and when the dust settled she spotted Nagle at the helm and an ashen-faced McClean stumbling from the passenger seat.

God, what had she let herself in for? What a motley crew. Morecamb was obviously a law unto himself and now she suspected that Nagle was the same. Murphy was a freak, she suspected McClean was on the spectrum. And Alderton.......well....she would reserve judgement on him. Surely it was only a matter of time before the lot of them was behind bars? In a way she hoped not because she had no desire to be here in any long-term capacity.

How had Nagle managed to negotiate the station's narrow entrance at that speed, in one piece? There was just the small matter of the 'Yield' sign which now lay smashed on the ground. But she would get McClean to sort that out.

Her thoughts were interrupted by a knock on the door and in trooped Morecamb with the speed merchant and his passenger.

"Thought you should hear this, Ma'am. Nagle and McClean have just arrived back from forensics. All yours, Nagle."

"Well, that's just it, there's nothing to tell, Ma'am. As soon as our forensic lads boarded the yacht a message arrived via the local plod telling them to stop the search. A specialised unit had been dispatched from Dublin and it would carry out the search."

"And who gave that message?" asked Thornhill.

"Wallace apparently and some young wretch from Kinsale passed it on. A Garda Harrington, I believe."

"Personally, I feel that this message warrants closer scrutiny," McClean piped up. "Both Inspector Morecamb and I are acquainted with this Harrington individual and whilst not wishing to cast aspersions…….."

"McClean, will you go out and fix up that 'Yield' sign before someone drives into it and sues us. Carry on, Morecamb."

Morecamb waited until McClean had glowered his way to the door and then continued where he had left off.

"Harrington is a twat," he confirmed, "but even he couldn't have mangled a simple message like, 'stop the search'. This whole thing is damned unethical. A member of that party, possibly even a suspect, decides who is going to carry out a search of the boat and when. And all the while he knows he will be questioned about the events on board. Do you know this Superintendent Wallace, Ma'am?"

"I don't know him personally but he's a pretty powerful man. Has the ear of Chief Commissioner O' Toole. But you still have a duty to carry out a thorough investigation even if it means rattling a few cages. Talk to that officer in Kinsale and find out what actually happened. Second-hand information is useless and doesn't carry much weight in an investigation."

"What's wrong with young McClean?" asked Morecamb as he left Thornhill's office with Nagle. "I thought he looked more pasty than usual."

"Ever been in a car with him?" asked Nagle.

"'Fraid so."

"What should have been a ten minute journey took half an hour."

"Sounds familiar."

"Bloody ridiculous. So I drove back. We actually made it in four and a half minutes. I wanted him to use the 'blues and twos' on the way out and he nearly wet himself. Anyway, fancy a pint? It must be nearly lunch-time."

"Just give me a minute. I want a word with Gwen. I'll catch you up in a sec."

*****

Gwen had been sitting at her desk for the past hour, trying to look busy. She had no intention of ringing any of Hunter's old cronies and was still trying to get her head around the enormity of the deception he had practised on her. Not 'practised' she thought bitterly. He was an expert. She fought back the tears as she remembered her initial enthusiasm about the pregnancy and then the awful reality when she had told him.

My God, she had even booked a table at a posh restaurant which she could ill-afford. A romantic dinner, she had whispered to him when they had bumped into one another in the corridor. They hadn't got past the bloody starter, she now bitterly recalled. And he couldn't get out of that restaurant fast enough. Just stayed long enough to tell her that it would have to end between them and he hoped she wasn't childish enough to cause any embarrassment to either of them.

"Any luck so far, Gwen?" Morecamb had suddenly appeared at her shoulder. "I know there's a Sergeant Gallagher in Store Street Garda Station. You could give him a call as well. Mrs Hunter is coming in at two so grab a bite to eat before that. See you later."

Gwen briefly considered giving this Gallagher man a call but she needed time to think. Of course she could have written the proverbial book on Hunter but she didn't want to show her hand so soon, if ever. But there was always the danger that the Garda Chief might mention the connection to Morecamb. But, considering the steps they had taken to expunge any connection between herself and 'the poor man', that seemed unlikely.

Still, she would have to show some evidence of her efforts. With a sigh she picked up the phone and dialled Store Street.

"Sergeant Gallagher, please."

"Speaking."

Gwen went on to give a brief explanation for her call.

"How is Inspector Morecamb? Tell him he owes me money. Long story but we had a bet. Must be two years ago. Tight git!" and his jolly laugh echoed down the phone. "Anyway, Hunter. Well, he was a bastard, God rest him. Did you know him at all? No, obviously not, otherwise you wouldn't be ringing me. Didn't see eye to eye with him to be honest. Always thought he was sly. Oh, a charmer I'm sure when it suited him. Always bragging about his contacts and important connections. Seemed to be no shortage of cash. Lived in a big house on Shrewsbury Road. I mean who the hell can afford a house there? Of course, I believe the wife's people are loaded but I heard they didn't have much time for him. Oh, and did I mention that I didn't like him?"

Gwen felt a whole lot better after the conversation and quickly made a note of the salient points; bastard, sly, boastful, corrupt, despicable, snob, sycophant. There! That would do for starters.

CHAPTER 9

Mrs Hunter was surprisingly young; that was Gwen's initial impression. Tall and willowy with translucent skin and long black hair. Would probably be considered attractive, If you liked that sort of look, Gwen reflected rather morosely. And she didn't look a day over thirty. Gwen's age.

"My name is Detective Inspector Morecamb and this is Detective Cassidy.

She was dressed in a classic matching dress and coat; emerald green and a matching ring and necklace. And green shoes, all perfectly co-ordinated. Some people liked that look. Most of the fashion magazines raved about it and the famous designers stitched their creations onto the stick-thin models before they tottered up and down the various catwalks, like clothes hangers suddenly come to life. It certainly wasn't Gwen's idea of _____.

"Detective Cassidy? Gwen!" Morecamb's stern voice shuddered her out of her daydream and all at once she hated herself for her lapse in concentration. In front of her, Mrs Hunter oozed self-confidence and wealth and suddenly Gwen felt insignificant, anonymous.

Morecamb pointed at the notebook with raised eyebrows and Gwen hurriedly apologised and began to write.

"First of all may I offer you our condolences, Mrs Hunter. Em......I don't know your Christian name...."

"It's Olivia but you can call me Mrs Hunter."

There was a moment's silence and Morecamb was a little taken aback.

"Okay, as you wish. So, can you tell us a little about your late husband?"

"There's not much to tell, really." She spoke in clipped tones. "We were married for eight years. No children. I think my husband would have liked a son but I wasn't keen. Anyway, he had his career and I'm very involved in charity work. Parts of Dublin are full of hungry children, you know, crying out for a bite to eat."

Gwen thought sourly that her ring could have fed the entire city for a few weeks.

"And of course there is a new scourge now. Drugs. Terrible blight on our capital and they're coming into this country by the truck load," she tutted.

"And was your husband a regular sailor?"

"Oh, yes. He's been sailing since we married. I bought him his first boat as a wedding gift. In the beginning he probably took her out three or four times a year. But for the past twelve months or so it was more frequent."

"Did you ever go with him, Mrs Hunter?"

"Oh, no, I prefer dry land. I don't think he was a particularly good sailor…….well, you could say my reservations have been borne out. But some of his friends were fairly adept so…."

"Do you know any of the people who were on board with him when this tragedy happened?"

"Well, obviously I knew Inspector Lonergan and I met the Wallace man a few times at a few functions. Not my idea of fun but duty and all that nonsense."

"Can you think of anybody who may have held a grudge against your husband?"

There was a pause and for a split second Gwen wondered if Mrs Hunter's gaze had lingered on her. Or was it just her imagination?

"Are you suggesting that he was murdered?" she asked, a look of distaste marring her features, as if murder was the preserve of the lower classes and had no place in her milieu.

"Well, we have to look at all the possibilities, you understand," Morecamb replied.

"I see. Well, my parents hated him. Thought he was a gold digger. His own brother accused him of having an affair with his wife. Also claimed that he had cheated him out of a small fortune. Don't know which upset the brother more. Then there's a neighbour of ours who claimed that Geoffrey had deliberately driven over his dog and killed it."

Gwen looked down at the list she had compiled after the call with Gallagher. He seemed to have covered all angles, she mused.

"So, he didn't have many fans?"

"You could say that. Oh, there's his sister, Isabel. She was a fan. Thought the sun rose and set on him. She wouldn't hear a bad word said about him. They were as thick as thieves, to coin a phrase. She was his confidante."

Once again, Gwen wondered if Mrs Hunter was looking directly at her when she made that last statement.

"So, if there's nothing else, Inspector, I've a plane to catch and my driver is waiting. I'm going to Spain for a few days' R&R. I've found this whole experience rather draining."

"Certainly. If you could just write out the contact details of your parents and his siblings, that would be great. We will need to contact them.

"If you must but perhaps you should make an appointment to speak to my parents before you actually do that. They don't like to feel ambushed."

"And how do you propose we should do that?" he asked. "Phone them in advance to let them know that we want to speak to them by phone and then put the phone down before picking it back up again to speak to them?"

"I don't appreciate your tone, Inspector. Naturally I was under the impression that you would be courteous enough to actually visit them. But, perhaps a phone call would be best. They don't suffer fools gladly. And believe me when I say they don't have a very high regard for the forces of law and order. Right, is that all?"

"Thank you. And just let us know when you're back from your R&R. We may need to speak to you again."

Morecamb escorted her out to the front door and then returned to the interview room. Had he waited for just a few moments he would have noticed that Mrs Hunter had got into a sleek convertible, driven by a man who didn't possess even a passing resemblance to a chauffeur.

"What did you make of all that, Gwen?" asked Morecamb returning to Gwen. "She's a snippy bitch, isn't she? And she certainly isn't falling down with grief."

"Well, it sort of ties in with Sergeant Gallagher's assessment of him." She consulted her notes again. "I'm quoting here; 'bastard, sly, despicable, sycophant, corrupt, snob and detestable'".

This testimony was delivered with a fine dollop of venom and Morecamb considered the woman sitting beside him. And would Gallagher really have used the word, 'sycophant'?

"Oh, and I forgot to mention, you owe Sergeant Gallagher money."

Morecamb quickly excused himself and moments later he was standing in front of Thornhill's desk.

"Gwen Cassidy, Ma'am. Is there something I should know?"

"I've no idea what you're talking about."

"There's just something…..can't quite put my finger on it……"

"Is she incompetent? Lazy?"

"Nooooo."

"Abrasive, argumentative?"

"No, nothing like that."

"What then?"

"Well, when I asked for her opinion on Hunter she trotted out some bloodcurdling epitaphs. For a moment I thought she was describing Alderton."

"Did she say how she had arrived at those conclusions?"

"Well, Sergeant Gallagher in Store Street seems to be the source of some of it but….."

"There you go then. Now, what about Mrs Hunter? How did the interview go?"

"Well, I couldn't describe her as heartbroken. Not relieved exactly but certainly happy enough to continue with her life. She's off abroad for a few days."

"Is she a suspect if this doesn't turn out to be accidental?"

"Hard to say at this early stage. But I'm keeping an open mind."

"So, is it wise to let her out of our sight?"

"Well, I've nothing to hold her for at the moment."

"Just be careful," she said as she gestured towards the door.

As he headed back towards his office he heard footsteps behind him accompanied by the jingle of medals.

"A word, Morecamb. Go on, get inside."

Alderton was puce in the face and started to do short circuits of the room.

"Alderton, get on with it. I have work to do."

"Murphy! You'll have to get rid of him. I'll not tolerate his presence in my office a minute longer. He's not even house-trained."

"Take it up with Superintendent Thornhill."

"Acting Superintendent, actually and I'm taking it up with you. It's your fault for the way he is." The digits appeared. "One, disobedient; two, incompetent; three, physically repulsive; four and five, he now has a cold and is spreading his own peculiar brand of germs all over my space. And not a handkerchief in sight!" Alderton finished on a roar.

"Come with me, Detective," said Morecamb as he stomped out of his office. He immediately headed for the interview room recently vacated by the Mrs Hunter. Thankfully Gwen was still there, busily writing in her notebook.

"Sit there, Sergeant."

"I'll sit where I like," snapped Alderton, "and I'm still a Superintendent so I'd like you to remember that."

"Not during this investigation, you're not. Sergeant Cassidy, this is Sergeant Alderton, one of the jolly sailors. Now, Alderton, we want to ask you a few questions about your seafaring escapade."

"Shouldn't I have legal whatsitcalled?"

"You're not under arrest, Sergeant Alderton," said Gwen. "You're simply helping us with our enquiries." Fair play to her, thought Morecamb. She would soon put Alderton in his place.

"And who are you?"

"This is Sergeant Cassidy and she'll be taking you through the statement which you gave after the incident."

"Well," huffed Alderton, "this is all very irregular….."

"Yes, we thought the same thing," said Morecamb.

"I mean, a woman sergeant and all that……..do you even know what you're doing?"

Oh dear!

"So," smiled Gwen, "a man died under mysterious circumstances and not a particularly popular individual, from all accounts. Can you describe your relationship with him, please?"

"What?"

"When you were questioned about events your response was, 'How the fuck should I know? I had my head bent over a bucket watching my insides flying all over the place. And all the while I was sitting on the toilet waiting for the rest of me to disappear into the sewage system.'" There was distaste etched on Gwen's face. "But none of that precludes you from some involvement in the events which unfolded. Can someone verify any of this?"

Alderton couldn't make up his mind on which one of them was more deserving of his disdainful scowl. He settled on Cassidy.

"Now, listen, Miss….."

"It's Sergeant Cassidy, Sergeant."

"Morecamb, tell her."

"Tell her, what?"

"That I'm a man above reproach, highly regarded, more years of service than anyone can count and a beacon in the entire community."

"Right, Sergeant Cassidy, you heard the man. Nobody has any idea how long he's been here. Part of the furniture. Now, Alderton, answer the question."

"What question?"

"Witnesses, Sergeant Alderton," replied Gwen.

"Are you bloody serious? Do you think I broadcasted the bloody thing? Maybe even sold tickets?" Alderton was practically levitating.

"So, no witnesses to your whereabouts," said Gwen calmly, making a note in her jotter. "And when did you first become aware that something had happened?"

"Not until the following morning, if you must know. It was all over by then."

"See, I find that hard to believe, Detective. A man drowns, there is consternation on board, lots of shouting and swearing we believe and you're seriously claiming complete ignorance."

"I wasn't a well man. Tell her, Morecamb."

"He's not a well man, Sergeant Cassidy. And completely ignorant."

Alderton paused to glare at Morecamb and then announced that he was going home to lie down. "So, if there's nothing else, Miss Cassidy?"

"Sit down, Alderton," said Morecamb. "We need to know what your relationship was like with Hunter".

"Well, obviously he held me in very high regard," puffed Alderton. "That goes without saying."

"And what about the other men?"

"Well, as you know I was good buddies with Superintendent Wallace, Inspector Lonergan and the late Superintendent Hunter. Similar rank, you understand. I can't say I ever met the other gentleman, Mr Cuthbert. Nice man, though. A little rough around _____."

"See, we'll have to stop you there, Alderton. There seems to be a level of disagreement regarding your man, Cuthbert. None of the others have mentioned him in their statements."

"That's impossible. Go back and read them again. Haven't I always told you about the importance of diligence?"

"No, I don't believe you've ever uttered the word in your life. Are you quite sure about this Cuthbert man?"

"Of course I bloody am. Wasn't I talking to him! He was certainly there. He had an English accent, a Londoner, I'm guessing, though from what he said I gather he has been all over the world. Which brings me back to that clown, Murphy, who hasn't been outside the county. Absolute savage of a man _____."

"But why have none of the others mentioned him, do you think?" asked Gwen.

Alderton looked flummoxed.

Morecamb began to wonder if Alderton had been on board at all. Was he just pretending that he was in such exalted company?

"You weren't by any chance just left on the quayside, Alderton?" he asked. "You know, just imagined the whole thing in your state of unwellness?"

"Don't be stupid."

"What is your last clear recollection of the trip, Sergeant?" Cassidy persisted.

"Well, the first day was splendid. Almost felt as if we weren't moving at all...."

"You weren't," snapped Morecamb.

"Shut up, Morecamb. Yes, everything was splendid. Good company, the most wonderful food, excellent wine, lots of banter and camaraderie."

"And how were you feeling that first night, Sergeant?"

"Perfectly fine, thank you. The sea was tranquil....that means calm, Morecamb. Excellent conditions."

"So, describe the next day. At what stage did you experience the internal combustion?" asked Cassidy.

"Well, I hardly think _____."

"Answer the question, Sergeant."

"I was fine until lunchtime, if you must know. Wonderful spread, lots of champagne." He smiled at the memory and then his features clouded over as he remembered his current stable companion. "He'll have to go, you know," he said, turning his scowl once more towards Morecamb.

"And how was the general atmosphere, Sergeant? Everybody getting along well?"

"Of course. We were a very civilised group of friends, enjoying each other's company......" He stopped, a frown creasing his forehead. "There was something....hard to put my finger on it....."

"Like a man being murdered?" asked Gwen, calmly.

"Don't be ridiculous. Look, Morecamb....."

"Answer the question, Alderton."

"Well, there may have been a little tension during the meal. A kind of lull in the conversation. I did my best, naturally, to restore everyone's spirits but not very successfully, as I recall....And then, I don't remember anything after the lunch. I can only assume that one of my friends must have helped me to my cabin....hopefully I hadn't shown my hand, so to speak, before I reached the toilet. My God, that would be unthinkable. The next thing I recall is the forensic gurriers shouting at me and ordering me off the yacht."

Alderton lapsed into a brooding silence and in spite of their best efforts he seemed incapable of answering any more questions. Without a backward glance he stalked out of the room.

CHAPTER 10

Thornhill called a quick meeting before they were due to knock off for the day.

"Right, let's have an update," she called.

Morecamb stood in front of the whiteboard and filled them in on the interview with Mrs Hunter. He refrained from calling on Gwen for a character reference on either Mrs Hunter or 'the dead man', as she was apt to call him. Strange that. Gwen had never referred to him by his name.

"So I'm afraid Mrs Hunter had very little information to advance the investigation. Alderton, however, is a different matter, as he usually is but he still claims that there were 5 of them on board and he's adamant that this Mr. Cuthbert was the fifth man. I'm still inclined to think that they left him behind, clutching his bucket and spade on the quayside. Even allowing for his seasickness, he surely didn't imagine the man. And yet, none of the others mentioned him. Any suggestions?"

"Is it possible," asked McClean, interrupting his neat writing and the construction of straight lines, "that Cuthbert was there and the others simply forgot because of all the trauma?"

"God knows. But the fact remains that none of the others mention anything at all about him. So somebody is lying. And there's another thing we need to check out........what did those forensic lads find, if anything."

"I'll chase that up," said Thornhill. "Rattle a few cages up there in Dublin."

"What about the pathology report?" asked Nagle. "I presume we got a copy of that."

"Not to my knowledge," said Thornhill.

"Well that's unusual too," said Morecamb. "What the hell are they playing at? This should have been a pretty straightforward investigation. Hunter wobbles off to his watery grave, helped in no small measure by the buckets of alcohol which he had consumed. Well, Jane is back at work tomorrow so I'll ask her to send over a copy of it."

"Jane?" queried Thornhill. "Who's Jane?"

"She's the Pathologist, Ma'am." Morecamb decided not to enlighten her any further on the girlfriend/boyfriend stuff. Anyway, it could all be in the trash-bin by this time tomorrow. "McClean and Gwen, will you two try to locate this Cuthbert character? Try the electoral register for starters. You never know your luck."

*****

Morecamb noticed that all the lights in his house were on as he pulled up in the drive-way.

Jane didn't do 'economy'.

And when he opened his front door he didn't get the tantalising aroma of food.

Jane didn't do 'cooking' either.

"Well?" she asked with a big grin on her face, "where are they?"

"Where are what?"

"My flowers, of course. As an apology."

"For what?" he frowned.

"For failing to defend my honour in JFK and allowing those Gestapo security officers to bully me."

"Give over!"

Suddenly she covered the distance between them and launched herself into his arms.

"Gotcha!" she laughed. "I've already forgiven you."

"Oh, that's a relief," he said as he hungrily kissed her.

"I've cooked dinner," she exclaimed when they eventually broke apart. "You can take that surprised look off your face," she teased as she led him by the hand into the kitchen.

"Ta-da!" She opened her arms wide, like a conjurer who had pulled not just one but two rabbits out of a hat. Certainly not the demeanour of somebody who was producing a plate of burned fish fingers and beans as the peak of their culinary achievement.

"That's amazing, Jane."

"Well……it's not much…." she began.

"No, seriously, it's bloody amazing. Unbelievable. If anybody had told me that it was possible to burn beans and fish fingers to a cinder _____."

"There's no need to go all cordon bleu on me, Jim Morecamb," she snapped. "If you spent your days dissecting bodies the last thing you'd want to cook is big slabs of meat."

They were suddenly interrupted by a loud banging on the door. Jane stomped off to answer it and arrived back, scowling, with Murphy in tow.

"Good evening, boss. Hope I'm not interrupting anything…."

"No, no, we're just discussing the merits of a meat-free diet."

"Would you like to join us, Sergeant?" Jane asked, though it sounded more like an order.

"Oh, God, yes please."

"There you go, you can have Jim's. He's not hungry apparently."

"Lovely," said Murphy as he peered at the burnt offering. "If you don't mind me asking….."

"Fish fingers and beans," snapped Morecamb, "eat up."

"Really?"

"Eat. If you don't it will still be here tomorrow night and the night after that," Morecamb muttered as he went over to the fridge and took out a beer "Anybody else?" he asked as he held up another bottle.

Jane ignored him and Murphy shook his head not wishing to prolong his visit any longer than was absolutely necessary.

"So, what brings you here, Murphy?" asked Morecamb, resuming his seat, "apart from an insatiable hunger."

"I'm your spy, remember?" said Murphy with his fork halfway to his mouth.

"A spy?" laughed Jane. "Who are you spying on? Is this even legal? Or ethical?"

"Cool it, Jane," said Morecamb. "We're the Gardai. We call it surveillance, all above board. It's how we catch criminals, remember? Go on, Murphy, before I lose interest."

"Right, well, he phoned his wife twice and she phoned him six times. And get this! She seemed to be suggesting that it might be a good idea if he had an affair with Superintendent Thornhill."

"Oh sweet Lord. Get out, Murphy. I asked you to do one simple task…."

"Shut up, Jim. Stay where you are, Sergeant. Who are we talking about here?"

"It's classified, Jane. For operational reasons we can't divulge that information. It isn't ethical."

"Who?" snapped Jane.

Murphy was torn between finishing whatever it was that had been served up to him and making a quick exit. There was also the issue of which of them he could safely ignore.

"Superintendent Alderton," stammered Murphy, "though of course he's only a Sergeant now so it's hardly….."

"One of your own?" asked Jane incredulously. "Why, in God's name? I know you don't like the man but this is outrageous behaviour."

"Look," said Morecamb, "I don't tell you how to do your job as a Pathologist _____."

"But, you could be putting Sergeant Murphy's life in danger. Have you thought of that? My understanding is that covert operations are only carried out by very skilled operatives _____."

"Tell you what, Jane," said Morecamb. "Why don't you do my job and I can grab the nearest cleaver and hack the next cadaver that arrives into the morgue into little pieces. How about that? Fair exchange is no robbery and all that."

Murphy hurriedly let himself out and furtively glanced over both shoulders as he hurried towards his car.

"What the hell is going on, Jim?" Jane asked when she realised they were on their own.

"I'm just trying to pacify Murphy, that's all," and he went on to tell her about Murphy's incarceration with Alderton and his indignation that he was being side-lined in the investigation into Hunter's death. "So, I'm the good guy here, Jane. Now, are you going to take me upstairs and ravish me?"

"If you're nice to me," she said, laughing over her shoulder as she ran ahead of him up the stairs.

The following morning Morecamb tentatively suggested that it might be a good idea if he asked his aunt Dot to cook a meal for them in the evenings. She lived only a mile away and he knew she would be only too glad to do it.

"I'm well able to cook," said Jane as she scraped the burnt bits off the toast over the kitchen sink. "Besides, your aunt doesn't like me. She blesses herself whenever she sees me."

"It's nothing personal, Jane. She just doesn't like your job. She believes bodies should be left intact.....well, so do I, for that matter, just when they're alive."

Eventually, albeit reluctantly, Jane agreed.

CHAPTER 11

There was silence in the Alderton household the following morning, with intermittent bouts of recriminations. Murphy's assessment of the constant phone calls of the previous day weren't so far wide of the mark. The morning had been preceded by a raucous evening, when they had sat on either side of the fireplace to have a civilised discussion. The topic had been Margie's insistence that her husband, the now defunct Superintendent, would have to take drastic steps to get himself reinstated as Superintendent and she had come up with a brilliant idea, according to herself.

Apparently blackmail was the way forward. He would have to consider circulating a rumour that he was having an extra marital affair with his replacement. Alderton wanted her to define the word 'extra' in that statement because to the best of his knowledge he wasn't the recipient of any existing marital affair.

There followed a long list of reasons why he was undeserving of any such attention and his recent demotion had put the kibosh on any such fanciful notions.

"And, might I remind you, my bags are still packed."

Tempting though that image was Alderton was adamant. He would not be circulating that rumour with a view to having Thornhill dismissed. And what was to stop his superiors in Dublin from dismissing him as well?

"Whoever heard of a man being dismissed for having an affair?" Margie asked, scornfully. "Don't be ridiculous". And she didn't let up until her husband promised to think about it.

Now, driving into work he was amazed by the sudden flash of inspiration which had suddenly assailed him. It struck with such force and it was such a novel experience that he nearly crashed the car. It had never happened before and he doubted if there would be a repetition.

He was going to order Murphy to spread a rumour that he, Murphy, was the beneficiary of Thornhill's affections, then, he could have Murphy sacked and get Thornhill moved.

God, he was good!

*****

Morecamb was in a good mood as well as he approached Union Quay Garda station. He had taken a detour on the way in, to call on his aunt and inveigle her into cooking dinner for him and Jane. She would be delighted, she said, because she felt that he had lost too much weight since the 'body-snatcher' had moved in with him.

Dot was in much better form these days, he thought. It had taken her a while to get over the death of her beloved Labrador, Holly and, in a moment of weakness, Morecamb had told her that she could 'borrow' his own dog, Willow, for a little while. That had been three months ago and, while his British Bulldog was always happy to see him, she showed no inclination to venture past the front door. And Dot wasn't offering.

As soon as he entered the station the desk sergeant told him that the Superintendent wanted to see him.

As usual Thornhill's door was open. She had told everybody that she would always be available as long as they didn't annoy her. Her predecessor on the other hand was fond of issuing threats and insults if they deigned to intrude on his sanctuary and, more often than not, they found his door locked when they approached it.

"Ah, good morning, Morecamb. Have a seat. I've been onto the Chief in Dublin and he seemed surprised that we wanted to be furnished with the inventory of the Forensic findings. I soon put him straight so he will get his secretary to fax it down to us. What about you?"

"Well, I've asked Jane to fax over the pathology report to us so hopefully we'll have that shortly. I also want to touch base with the others who were on board the boat or yacht or whatever it was. I don't fancy traipsing all the way up to Dublin though."

"Well, if you have to I'll organise a driver for you and you can stay overnight, if necessary. Mention the Shelbourne Hotel to them. That might bring them down here fairly sharpish. That will be all. Let me know what they say. Oh, and start with Lonergan. He's the more junior of the two."

*****

Murphy's life was flashing before his eyes. Alderton was unveiling his grand plan.

He had genuinely intended presenting it as a suggestion but then realised the folly of doing it that way. Because of Murphy's uncouth demeanour and total lack of any susceptibility to innuendo or subtlety, he had changed tack at the last minute. He was now issuing an edict.

"That is to say you have no choice, Murphy. I can safely say that both of our welfares depend upon this. And, while I could never be accused of vindictiveness, nevertheless I feel it only fair to point out to you that I will make your life a living hell if you fail me in this."

Murphy, no stranger to 'living hell' felt this was a step too far. And, even though it hadn't been spelt out, he knew that Alderton was trying to buy his silence. He just wasn't paying that much for it. In fact, nothing at all.

Well, thought Murphy, if Morecamb had been underwhelmed by the previous night's revelations, wait until he got a load of this! It was obvious that Alderton was up to his neck in the shenanigans in Kinsale and now he wanted him to.....what? Where did Superintendent Thornhill fit into all this? Well, he was sure that given time he could figure it out and present a credible narrative to Morecamb which wouldn't cause him to explode.

CHAPTER 12

When he left Thornhill's office Morecamb spotted Gwen and called her over.

"Gwen, I want you to ring Lonergan and set up a meeting with him. Tell him I need to speak to him about events in Kinsale. Make it for Tuesday. It's a Bank holiday weekend so no point in trying to arrange anything before next week. Don't say too much to him, just keep it vague. I want to have a chat with McClean and Nagle so will you join us in the Incident Room when you're finished?"

"Yes, sir."

Gwen returned to her desk deep in thought. Had she ever seen Lonergan while she was in Hunter's company, say in the canteen or even in his office? She didn't think so. And she doubted Hunter would have said anything. In fact she was fairly sure he hadn't. Just went snitching to the Chief Commissioner!

When she rang Dublin she got no further than Lonergan's secretary.

'Of course she couldn't speak to Inspector Lonergan! She would have to make an appointment to speak to him but, as his secretary, she would need to be apprised of the nature of the call. How else could she determine if the matter was urgent?'

"No," Gwen replied, "the matter is highly confidential."

"Well, in that case I think he has a vacant spot on Tuesday week."

"Fantastic. Just tell him that it concerns his role in a possible murder in Kinsale. Good girl."

Gwen smiled as she replaced the receiver. "Tuesday week? I think not," she muttered. Just as she was about to head into the Incident Room the phone rang again.

*****

"So, McClean, any luck in tracking down this Cuthbert man?"

"No, sir. When I admitted that I didn't know his Nationality, date of birth or address they put the phone down on me. I did get through to Wallace's secretary, though and she said she'd ring me back with the info this morning. And when she did the message was short and to the point. Wallace knew absolutely nothing about him."

"Well, hopefully we'll be interviewing Lonergan soon so we'll ask him. Ah, Gwen, how did you get on?"

"Not very well, sir. Inspector Lonergan is too busy to talk to anybody but he has a free slot on Tuesday week and he can fit you in then."

Morecamb's face went a dark purple and McClean wondered if Cassidy might benefit from a course on how best to deliver bad news without triggering an explosion………

"The secretary said what?" bellowed Morecamb.

Gwen stood her ground.

"Would you like me to repeat it, sir?"

…..or how to put the pin back in the grenade without blowing the entire room to smithereens, McClean ruminated.

"Would you like me to try?" asked McClean and Nagle closed his eyes and counted to five.

"What do you mean, McClean?" exploded Gwen. "Are you suggesting that you're more capable than I am…."

"Urgent phone call, sir," said Garda Moloney, poking his head around the door and then hurriedly withdrawing.

"There's one other thing, sir," began Gwen……..

"It can wait. I'll be back in a few minutes."

"Morecamb here," he announced as he picked up the phone. "Who's this?"

48

"Inspector Lonergan. I've just had a scurrilous message delivered to my good self, courtesy of your secretary, I presume. Might I remind you that I've already provided a full and frank statement on the events surrounding the unfortunate incident in Kinsale."

"Your statement was neither full nor frank, Inspector. So please make yourself available here on Tuesday, at eleven o' clock."

Lonergan pointed out that he couldn't possibly do that. He would be attending a friend's funeral in London, not that it was any of Morecamb's business and he wouldn't be back for three or four days. And it had all been cleared with his Superiors so if Morecamb had a problem with that he knew who to speak to.

The exchange did not help Morecamb's mood and when Gwen delivered her second piece of news it took a catastrophic nosedive.

"Jane rang, sir, just after I was on to Inspector Lonergan's secretary. She said she'd tried your direct line but you weren't picking up. Anyway, she asked me to pass on a message."

Oh boy, here we go, thought McClean.

"She said she couldn't locate any pathology report on the dead man and when she asked her lab assistant he said that it was the Chief State Pathologist who had carried out the P.M. You'll have to go through the proper channels, she said."

Oh, oh.

"I can handle that, Inspector," said Nagle. "I used to date a lassie whose brother works in the lab in Dublin."

"Great. Gwen, will you ask Superintendent Thornhill if she had any luck chasing down forensics and then put all the information we have on that incident board. Lonergan is fecking off to some funeral in London and won't be back for a few days, though who would want him at their funeral is a mystery. But, don't worry, we'll catch him later. McClean, you're with me. We're going to take a trip down memory lane. We'll see you all on Tuesday morning."

CHAPTER 13

Kinsale hadn't changed. There was no reason why it should have, of course. It had been more than a year since they had been involved in a murder investigation here and this was Morecamb's first trip back. As they drove by the rolling green fields Morecamb began to relax. He rolled down the window and breathed in the wonderful smells and sounds.

"The restorative powers of nature, McClean. You can't beat it."

There was very little traffic and, as they negotiated each twist in the road, nature seemed to offer up an ever-changing vista. There was something about nature that seemed to get it right every time, Morecamb mused. Animals quietly just kept their head down and chewed every blade of grass in their path. No squabbling over who had the right of way or who had first dibs on a particular patch of grass. Each just lumbered along in their own sweet way. No territorial battles, no pangs of conscience about right and wrong, no sudden burst of madness culminating in one of their number beating another about the head and leaving him for dead. He had read somewhere that cows have three stomachs. Murphy would be impressed.

"Would you like to be a cow, McClean?" Morecamb asked, turning to his companion.

McClean had hoped that with his more stable home situation that Morecamb might start to behave like a normal human being but he was obviously getting madder by the minute. And he certainly wasn't going to dignify that question with an answer. Besides, whatever answer he gave would be the wrong one. So he kept his eyes on the road and pretended that he hadn't heard.

As they slowed to enter the town of Kinsale another kind of beauty awaited. They had detoured, on Morecamb's insistence, by the Old Head and the sea unveiled a new beauty. It seemed quite choppy today but he could still spot the hardy fishermen, like dots, in the distance. The waves seemed to ebb and flow and he marvelled at the expertise of those men who seemed unconcerned as they battled their old foe though he was quite sure that they had plenty of reason to be grateful to it too. Like a lover, generous one minute and greedy the next. That gave and sometimes took away.

McClean was engrossed in his own thoughts. He hadn't been back here either and that saddened him. A distant relation owned a summer house in Garretstown and McClean and his mother had been invited to stay, twice. He had dreamed of having his own place there at some stage in the future but events surrounding those murder investigations last year had left a sour taste. The whole thing had been quite unsavoury, culminating in an ill-advised swim off Garretstown which in turn had led to a period in, what could be termed, solitary confinement.

"Happy memories, McClean?" asked Morecamb as they pulled up outside the barracks.

"Not many. In fact, none at all. I used to enjoy trips here with the folks but last year ruined all that."

"Right, well, let's see who's on the welcoming committee this time."

As soon as they stepped inside the door there was a flurry of excitement and Garda Harrington launched himself at Morecamb and enveloped him in a bear hug. Sergeant McGrath followed at a more sedate pace but his welcome was no less sincere. He shook both men's hands and ushered them into his office.

Yes, he was now a detective and young Harrington had been promoted to Sergeant.

McClean looked crestfallen at this piece of news and Morecamb could almost see the cogs turning. How in God's name could such a half-wit occupy the same rank as himself? Morecamb was inclined to share those sentiments but, perhaps with the steadying hand of McGrath to steer him, Harrington would be okay. As long as he didn't take to the drink or decide to go rogue and take it upon himself to try to solve a crime. Any crime at all.

"I believe you had a bit of excitement last week, McGrath?"

"You could say that. There was even more excitement immediately following the event."

"In what way? Can you take us through it?"

"Well, I wasn't actually on duty though I came as quickly as I could. I was in Cork, you see, visiting an aunt of mine in hospital."

"Allow me, Detective McGrath," said Harrington, stepping forward.

Oh God, thought Morecamb and McClean, simultaneously. McGrath probably as well.

Yes, Harrington was indeed the sole representative of the Garda Siochana when there was an urgent message delivered from the Harbour Master.

Morecamb was quite sure there was no such person.

It took Harrington a little while to find his cap and he couldn't locate the car keys so he had to jog to the harbour. Just as well that he had been quite the sprinter in school _____.

"Get to the point, Harrington," snapped Morecamb.

"Well, when I arrived there was a lot of shouting, even hysteria….."

"And you waded in and made things worse," said Morecamb. "Yes, we get that. Get on with it."

"There were very important men on board so I was told to move the crowd back. Now, that wasn't easy because _____."

"Who told you to move the crowd back?"

"Well, one of the important gentlemen on board. Showed me his ID. A Superintendent no less _____."

"And then?"

"Well, it was kind of straightforward really. There was Superintendent Wallace on board _____."

"We know."

"Oh, right. Anyway, he was really helpful and told me to guard the scene while he came up here to make some phone calls. And, my God, didn't a newspaper reporter arrive and wanted to know what had happened. I told him I had no idea. And do you know what he wrote in his newspaper the following morning?" added a deeply offended Harrington.

Morecamb did. Thornhill had already informed him.

'CHAOS STRIKES AGAIN,' the headline had screamed and the accompanying article had made various references to 'overwhelmed', 'chaos' (3 times), 'lack of direction', full details of an earlier murder investigation in the town and how the locals had been subjected to the mother and father of all horrors during that one.

Thornhill had also been contacted by a representative of the local businesses, whinging about the reputational damage to the great and the good and all the commercial outlets, "selling tat", Thornhill had added.

"So, I immediately decided to contact Detective McGrath," Harrington rattled on, "and then _____."

"Go back," interrupted Morecamb, "do you mean that you left the harbour, unattended, and drove back to the barracks to call McGrath?"

Harrington stopped, wondering which part of the narrative had caused the consternation. And then it dawned on him.

"Oh, yes. No, I didn't drive. Remember, I told you about losing the car keys so I ran as fast as I could though I must say my time wasn't as good as _____."

"So, when he contacted me at the hospital I came straight away," McGrath put in, sensing a sharp deterioration in the atmosphere.

"And, believe it or not," interrupted Harrington, "didn't I find the car keys.............." His voice petered out as he saw the look on Morecamb's face.

"And then?"

Well, things had calmed down considerably, he was glad to say. Superintendent Wallace, a very nice man, took some statements from those on board, hurriedly wrote up his own and said he would take charge of everything.

One of the other men on board, an Inspector Lonergan, went straight back to Dublin to report the incident there. Poor man was exhausted. So there was only Superintendent Wallace and half the townspeople hanging around.

His listeners very gingerly sat down on the nearest available chairs and Harrington felt it was marvellous to have such an attentive audience.

"Then, Superintendent Wallace very kindly offered to get me a flask of tea while I stood guard over the yacht. We didn't want any unauthorised personnel on board, the Superintendent said. So I spent the next hour or so _____."

"Where do you fit into all this, McGrath?" asked Morecamb in an ominously quiet voice.

"Well, when I arrived back an hour or two later _____."

"Were you walking?" snapped Morecamb.

"Two and a half hours, actually," Harrington piped up. "See I took note of everything."

McGrath glared at his sergeant and decided to steer well clear of Harrington's narrative of the most appalling ineptitude. Anyway, it wasn't his fault and he was damned if he was going to be implicated in any way so he kept silent. If he didn't say anything then Morecamb, who seemed transfixed by young Harrington's unfolding tale, might forget he was even there.

Meanwhile Harrington was rattling off the series of events, in no discernible order; Superintendent Alderton wasn't discovered until the following morning and was too ill to give a statement; the Forensic crew was from Dublin as was the Forensic Photographer; Superintendent Wallace had organised all that, "fair play to him" because by now all the locals were milling around, "some in their pyjamas and wellingtons and didn't I say to you later, Detective McGrath, that it was like a scene from Jaws? And when we got back to Kinsale after bringing Superintendent Alderton home it was as if nothing at all had happened. Superintendent Wallace was gone, the yacht was gone, the locals _____."

"Shut up, Harrington," said McClean, beginning to dread the return journey to Cork with Morecamb.

"You shut up, McClean," retorted Harrington. "Remember, I'm the same rank as you are and I'm entitled to the same respect."

McClean scowled at him and was tempted to give him a taste of the kind of respect to which he was subjected on a regular basis back in Cork.

"We dropped the statements off at Union Quay," McGrath offered, deciding that the worst was probably over and hoping that the two from Cork would clear off. "We gave them to Sergeant Murphy, as he seemed to be in charge, though he strenuously denied it."

"So, let me get this straight," said Morecamb. "Am I right in saying that the entire incident was managed by the very people who might well prove to be the main suspects?"

Even Harrington suspected that now might be the right time to keep quiet and McGrath was, once again, staring off into the middle distance and visualising the medicinal malt which he kept in a drawer, for emergency occasions such as this.

Morecamb scraped back his chair, announced they were leaving and beckoned to McClean.

As soon as they were in the car Morecamb turned to McClean and ordered him not to utter a word for the duration of the journey.

McClean was only too happy to oblige. Thank God for the long weekend.

CHAPTER 14

Gwen braced herself. It was time to go into Thornhill's office and enquire about the Forensic results. When she had tried on Friday Thornhill had been nowhere in sight. She'd been surprised by that because, in Dublin, she was often the last to leave. But Gwen was beginning to sense the tension in this station. At times you could practically cut the atmosphere with a knife.

She knew that, as a woman, Superintendent Thornhill wasn't universally welcomed. The Murphy fellow was going around like a scalded cat. Alderton was obviously the most put out and the chest full of medals that he sported was a feeble kick-back at the turn of events. As far as Gwen could see nobody was in the slightest bit impressed with his display and most regarded the jingle as he swaggered up and down the corridors as a mere irritant. Morecamb of course seemed to be in an eternal state of near combustion but he didn't faze Gwen. She had dealt with the insidious bullying of an entire department in Dublin and in fairness to Morecamb there was nothing underhand about him and his wrath seemed to be directed at those who were incompetent and could prove an impediment to the progress of the investigation.

As soon as Gwen reached Thornhill's office to check on the Forensic results she immediately sensed something was wrong. For starters Thornhill wasn't at her desk. She then noticed that the blinds were hanging drunkenly to one side and there seemed to be an abundance of files scattered around the place. She went over to straighten the blind and when she looked out onto the enclosed courtyard at the back she spotted thick plumes of smoke rising into the air. As she peered closer she saw Thornhill sucking rather desperately on a cigarette and, even though it was a long way down, she could have sworn that she had two lighted cigarettes on the burn.

After another minute another figure emerged through the back door. Alderton. His face lit up when he spotted Thornhill. She reached out and offered him the second cigarette and the two of them stood, side by side, companionably blowing smoke rings into the air. Gwen beat a hasty retreat to the incident room and decided she would try Thornhill again in half an hour. It was either that or face the wrath of Morecamb when he came in.

She decided to give it an hour and then she approached Thornhill's door again. This time the experience was even more unsettling. The Superintendent was calmly sitting at her desk, with a cloth in her hand and was assiduously cleaning a pistol. She waved Gwen into a chair and spent the next few minutes focussed on the gun.

"Do you think the muzzle of this looks slightly off focus?" Thornhill asked.

"God, no," blurted Gwen hoping she would put it back in its case and praying it wasn't loaded. "Inspector Alderton…..sorry, I mean Morecamb asked me to find out if you'd heard anything back……It's just we were wondering if you had any update…."

"Forensics, right?" interrupted Thornhill. "No. Uncooperative. I'm expecting a herd of sharp-suited lawyers any moment now and, hopefully, my Union representative. I may have threatened the powers that be with exposure to the Minister. How are you getting on with Morecamb?"

Gwen's head was beginning to spin.

"He seems….."

"You're going to say 'nice' or 'fine', aren't you? Listen, Gwen, I know it's difficult starting off again in a new station. It's new for me too. We women have to stick together. Remember, we're in a man's world. You know, we should go out for a drink together. Sometimes," she sighed, "I wish I was back in New York."

Actually, she often wished she was back but there was the small matter of a huge debt which she owed to some rather unsavoury characters whose regular visits had turned more threatening in the months preceding her departure. Their reach was wide, necessitating a change of name when she reached this side of the pond and facilitated, in no small way, by her Uncle in the department. So, she had assumed her mother's maiden name and consigned the name 'Beecher' to the past. Only in the middle of the night did it resurface, forcing her from her bed to stare wide-eyed out the window as she waited for the dawn.

"It must seem strange to you, Gwen", she continued, "but I feel quite nostalgic when I hold this gun. Sometimes I wish the Garda here carried firearms. I think it would, for the most part, make their jobs easier. We certainly couldn't survive without them in the States. Alright, maybe sometimes we get it wrong but I truly believe that it balances out in the end. And I know Superintendent Alderton feels the same. Anyway, enough about extolling the virtues of a loaded gun. Now, was that all you wanted?"

"Yes, Ma'am, I think so."

"Good. Close the door on your way out."

Later, in the canteen, Detective Nagle plonked his tray down on the table and sat across from Gwen.

"Okay, you first, Cassidy."

"Well, there's not a lot to tell. Actually, that's a lie," she said as she chased a sausage around her plate. When she eventually stabbed it with her fork and set about chopping it up with the gusto which was usually the preserve of a demented butcher, Nagle pushed his chair back a little. "She has a gun you know."

"Who are we talking about?" Nagle asked, looking around and wondering if he was in danger from several angles.

"The Superintendent," Gwen supplied. "She has a loaded pistol in there."

"Right. Did she give an explanation?"

"I gather she's expecting a few lawyers and some representative from the Union."

"Mmm….that doesn't sound good. I know she has no time for the Union representative. What's his name…..Collopy, that's it. Nearly came to blows the last time their paths crossed."

"Oh. Is he a regular visitor?"

"'Fraid so. She thinks lawyers are on temporary release from hell, to give the Devil some head space. Maybe we should have the Rapid Response Unit on standby," he laughed as he investigated the meat in his steak and kidney pie.

"Anyway I gather she hadn't much luck with the lads in Dublin regarding the forensic results", Gwen continued. " And I think I'm safe in saying that the chaos in her office was triggered in no small way by the exchange. Files all over the place and the blinds look as if they had been attacked."

"I think this case is becoming more complicated by the day," Nagle said. "I got in touch with my contact in Pathology earlier this morning. He told me he'd make enquiries and get back to me. Got a call from him just before I came in here and he said the Pathology results seem to be under lock and key. Nobody up there has seen them so they haven't even been logged into the central system. It seems to me that there are two separate investigations going on and one side is holding all the cards. And they're in no hurry to share them."

They were just finishing up their lunch when Morecamb came through the doors. McClean followed up looking sulky and most put out. He still hadn't recovered from Friday's escapade and Morecamb's rant all the way back to Cork, in spite of the fact that he had promised there would be no talk.

"Stay where you are," called Morecamb as he spotted the two diners making preparations to leave. McClean didn't bother going up to the counter and sat down straight away and started to eat an apple.

"No major breakthrough in Kinsale then?" asked Nagle.

McClean seemed to be in a world of his own and ignored the question.

"We're going to have an emergency meeting after this," said Morecamb as he slapped his tray down on the formica-topped table. "McClean, put that apple in the bin and get yourself something normal to eat. I'm going to ask Superintendent Thornhill to join us. Gwen, you go into her and tell her. But give her a few minutes," he continued. "I just saw a pack of lawyers fuming past in the corridor and, if I'm not mistaken, a tearful Union representative."

Just then McClean arrived back with a banana and a cup of coffee so Gwen decided that now might be a good time for a trip to the Superintendent's office.

*****

Thornhill was like a caged animal at the top of the room as Morecamb called the meeting to order.

"Summarising the details of this case won't take long," he began. "There was the usual cock-up in Kinsale where one of the main witnesses, Superintendent Wallace, seems to have taken complete charge of the entire proceedings while one newly-promoted Sergeant Harrington was attempting to break Bannister's mile record. On the other hand, Detective McGrath took three hours to make the journey from Cork to Kinsale and he assured me that he wasn't walking. Nagle, take us through your conversation with our brethren in Dublin, please."

Nagle's report was succinct. He hadn't even bothered to stand up for his delivery, such was its brevity and the paucity of information.

"And what about yourself, Superintendent? You spoke to forensics, is that right?"

Thornhill's report was simply an astonishing explosion of libellous references to all and sundry up in Dublin. She then segued to a volley of malicious invective directed at the lawyers who had been recently dispatched with the threat of extinction, along with the Union Rep, for good measure.

The upshot was that the secretary had enumerated Forensic's very rudimentary findings over the phone and there wouldn't be any follow-up.

A long silence followed Thornhill's delivery with a wide gamut of reactions, ranging from admiration to fear.

Morecamb was the first to break the silence and while his tone lacked the demented ranting of Thornhill it was no less effective and, in its own way, just as menacing. Unfortunately, it was at this moment that a hapless Murphy had decided that now might be a good time to have an open and frank discussion about his personal safety, in view of his new role as a spy. But as soon as he put his head around the door both Thornhill and Morecamb screamed at him to get out so he beat a hasty retreat.

"O' Toole is the head honcho in headquarters, isn't he," asked Morecamb.

"Yes," sighed Thornhill.

"Well, couldn't you ask him…."

"We're not on speaking terms," Thornhill snapped.

"Since when?"

"As of this morning. I explained to him that we were having difficulty accessing the forensic report. So he asked me if he should send a replacement Superintendent…. a man who would have had a full report on his desk as of yesterday. To my credit I said, 'no thanks', and then I might have threatened to complain him to the highest level. So you could say that avenue is now closed. Hence, the lawyers."

"And you had no luck either with your contact in pathology, Nagle?"

"None."

"Right," said Morecamb, "let's do this our way and to hell with discretion and all that nonsense. We're going to lean on Lonergan and Wallace and forcibly extract the information."

"But, Morecamb, we're working on the basis that the drowning was accidental," warned Thornhill. "Of course it would be nice to think that somebody had decided to dispatch the horrible man but we really don't have any evidence."

"Be that as it may, Superintendent, but they're still trying to hamper our enquiries and some of their actions to date have been highly unorthodox. So, as of now we take complete control. Any questions? No? Good."

*****

Morecamb almost felt giddy as he opened his front door and the aroma of steak filled his nostrils. When he went into the kitchen Jane was busy laying the table, a disapproving scowl marring her features.

"You know I don't approve of meat," she began, "and your aunt bloody knows that too. So I want you to leave a note on the table in the morning where she'll see it and tell her that meat is off the menu from now on."

"So what's with the second lot of cutlery then?"

"Well, as there is nothing else to eat I have no choice. But I'll just eat the vegetables."

"Good idea. Do you want a beer?"

They ate their meal in silence and in spite of her aversion to meat Jane had a second helping of the casserole cooked by Aunt Dot.

"It's not that I'm ungrateful," said Jane as she finished the last morsel, "but do leave a note in the morning asking her to cook fish instead."

"You've either had a very rough day or else it's been boring and you would welcome a face-off with my aunt. Besides, we only eat fish on a Friday as a form of punishment. Something to do with the Catholic Church."

"Jim, you could pretend….."

"No."

"….that you've turned vegetarian since our trip to America."

"No way."

"And that as I'm pregnant I find the sight of meat hard to stomach."

"WHAT!" screamed Morecamb.

"Just saying," said Jane calmly.

"Just saying, what?"

"Since our trip stateside…."

"Not that bit, for God's sake!"

"Well, lots of people are starting to turn vegetarian so why _____."

She was interrupted by a loud banging on the front door. Morecamb didn't think his legs would support him as far as the door. When he was making no move to budge Jane patted her stomach and nodded towards the hall.

It was Murphy.

He didn't wait for an invitation but barged straight into the kitchen.

"Boss, you're not going to believe this _____."

"Pregnant, are you, Murphy?"

"What?" Murphy turned to Jane for clarification but she, in turn, was busy scowling at her partner.

"Murphy, say your piece but only if it's relevant to the investigation."

A more astute individual would have immediately assessed the situation and made an immediate exit but Murphy wasn't blessed with any such intuitive streak. So he sat down and beamed across the table at Jane.

"Any chance of a cup of tea and maybe a sandwich?"

A frosty silence greeted the request.

"Right. Anyway, boss, I know you weren't very impressed with my report last night but wait 'til you hear this _____."

"No, Murphy, I'm not going to wait for anything. Spit it out."

So Murphy relayed the morning's saga to his astonished audience and when he came to the part where he decided to mention his own bizarre interpretation of Alderton's manoeuvrings Morecamb announced that he was going upstairs to get his gun. He clattered off upstairs at a speed which belied his 42 years of a rather sedentary life but matched, if not exceeded, by the speed of Murphy's exit.

CHAPTER 15

Morecamb's journey to the station the following morning was calmer than he might have predicted the previous night. Jane had confessed that she was only joking about the pregnancy and she couldn't for the life of her understand why he didn't see the funny side of it. Morecamb had gone on to cite Murphy's words of wisdom on the subject, that parenthood was a state to be avoided at all costs and it was so dire that Murphy hoped to have retired before his daughter reached 16. If not he could visualise having to arrest her for anti-social behaviour and public affray. Along with her mother no doubt.

Jane reminded him that he would probably be gaga when their child reached that age which took them onto the subject of fish and its beneficial qualities for a long and healthy life.

In the end he had to promise that he would broach the subject with Aunt Dot. As there was no deadline he decided he could put it on the long finger.

As soon as he went into the station he headed straight for Thornhill's office and told her that he and Nagle were going to Dublin immediately to interview Wallace.

"And what about Lonergan?"

"Unfortunately, he's away in London for a few days. Something about a funeral."

"Why not get Wallace down here?"

"Well, if we bring Wallace here he'll be lawyered up and we won't get a word out of him. So I think we should surprise him and talk to him on his own turf."

"And what if he refuses to see you?"

"Then I have every intention of going to the Deputy Commissioner O' Toole".

"Despicable man….."

"Be that as it may, I'm still going to talk to him if I get no joy from Wallace. It's seven now so we will be able to make the eight o' clock train."

When he found Nagle he told him about the plan and, as he headed towards his office he spotted Murphy coming through the front door laden down with an armful of dry-cleaners. He hurried to open the door of Alderton's newly-requisitioned office for him and then followed Murphy inside. Alderton was on the phone and did a double-take when he saw Morecamb.

Murphy dumped the clothes across the back of a chair which immediately tumbled onto the floor under the strain. Alderton dropped the phone and reached for his baton but the scowl on Morecamb's face stayed his hand.

"Murphy, grab a chair and come over here," ordered Morecamb.

There was a strangled squeal from Alderton as his room-mate ditched the polythene- wrapped suits, righted the chair and sat beside Morecamb in Alderton's direct line of venom.

"I have a job for both of you………."

"Naturally we shall not be complying."

"…..relating to 'the disgraceful incident in Kinsale', to quote Deputy Commissioner O' Toole……."

"He said no such thing!"

"………..on whom I am calling today," Morecamb ploughed on.

"We only deal in cold cases here, Morecamb."

"*Detective Inspector* Morecamb. I want both of you to find out as much as you can about Inspector Lonergan and Superintendent Wallace, your sea-faring buddies, Alderton."

"I repeat, *'cold cases'.*

"We need to gather as much information as possible on the main players in Kinsale which is sketchy at best especially if this turns into a murder investigation."

"Jesus wept".

As soon as the door closed behind Morecamb Alderton sprang into action and Murphy was ordered to retrieve the clothes from the floor and bring them straight back to the dry cleaners to be re-pressed.

CHAPTER 16

The train to Dublin was packed and it wasn't until they reached the station in Portlaoise that Morecamb and Nagle secured a seat. It was a silent journey for the most part as Morecamb was still mulling over Murphy's 'great reveal' and wondered what kind of monster he'd unleashed when he'd asked his sergeant to do him a small favour.

On a perverse whim Morecamb decided they would have breakfast in the Shelbourne hotel, the full Irish, charged to Garda Headquarters and then they enjoyed a leisurely stroll over to Store Street Garda station.

The reception area of the station was manic. Morecamb was surprised, considering it wasn't even the weekend yet. Young whelps who had overindulged the night before were scattered about the place and whose mothers, for the most part, had been summoned to sign them out. They could hardly wait to get their 'disgraceful' sons off the premises before giving them a few clatters across the head. Some didn't even wait until they reached the anonymity of the street before lambasting them about their uselessness and their uncanny resemblance to their old man who had buggered off before the son had taken his first steps and hadn't been seen since.

As Morecamb looked around he could almost see the broken promises and harsh realities in the faces of the main players while a few floors up crimes of a far greater magnitude probably festered undetected.

He and Nagle stood back and waited as hastily scribbled signatures adorned release documents and meagre possessions were handed over. A handful of gum-chewing lassies trooped past, tottering on their high heels and eye-popping mini-skirts and gave a cheeky wink to the two men as they giggled past them.

No doubt they would all be back by the weekend. It was the nature of the beast and they all had had a 'brilliant night.'

Eventually, when things had quietened down a little Morecamb approached the desk sergeant and asked to see Superintendent Wallace.

"Do you have an appointment?"

Morecamb produced his warrant card and the sergeant hastily picked up the phone and dialled an internal extension. After a few moments a deep frown marked his features and he glanced furtively under his eyebrows at his two guests. Finally he put his hand over the receiver and whispered, "Em…. he's quite busy now and says you'll have to make an appointment."

"Give me the phone, please," said Morecamb.

"Em, I wouldn't do that, sir. Right, ok, no problem," he relented as the receiver was snatched out of his hand.

There was a terse exchange down the line but the sergeant noticed that the word 'murder' seemed a deciding factor and Morecamb and Nagle walked smartly through the internal door and, much to the relief of the sergeant, disappeared into the bowels of the building. He was almost friendly to the next toe-rag who was being released from his over-night stay in the cells.

"How do we approach this, Boss?" asked Nagle as they neared Wallace's lair.

"How about we play it by ear? Let's see what kind of reception we get though judging from my encounter on the phone I'm not hopeful. But we'll see."

Wallace's secretary answered their knock, opened the door and immediately skidaddled back to her own little cubby hole of an office.

There was no greeting from Wallace. He simply leaned back in his chair and observed them coolly. They sat, uninvited, on the two chairs in front of his desk.

"Well, gentlemen," he smirked, "I'm afraid you've come an awfully long way on a wasted journey."

"Oh, we'll be the judge of that, sir," Morecamb replied, maintaining eye contact all the time. "Our next stop is Deputy Commissioner O' Toole so you could say we've covered all angles. In the unlikely event of any deliberate prevarication or obstruction from your good self we took the precaution of making a few more appointments. See, we've come a long way and we don't want a wasted journey. Detective Nagle, would you care to start proceedings?"

Wallace's face flushed a deep, angry crimson.

"Nagle?" queried Wallace with raised eyebrows. "Your reputation precedes you. Got rid of you, did they?"

"Not really, sir," replied Nagle, calmly. "Put in for a transfer actually. I was hoping to have a gentle lead-in but then this mess landed. Still, gives me the chance to mingle with the great and the good and, who knows, I might get the chance to watch an edifice or two crumble," he finished with a broad smile. "Shall I begin, Inspector Morecamb?"

"Be my guest".

"Okay, we'll start with the easy question. Who was on board the sailing expedition and could I have their names and rank, please," began Nagle.

"Look, I've already given _____."

"We'll come to that later, sir. Names and rank, please?"

Wallace threw his eyes to heaven and barked out, "Superintendent Hunter, my good self, Alderton, Inspector Lonergan. Are we done now?" he snapped.

"Not quite, sir. We've been reliably informed that there was a further guest, a Mr. Cuthbert."

"Never heard of him."

"Then why is one of the aforementioned adamant that there was a fifth member?"

"Look, there was a fair amount of alcohol involved. And I trust your source is one Superintendent Alderton though I believe he has been demoted."

"Temporarily," said Morecamb.

"Gentlemen," said Wallace leaning forward, "there was no Mr. Cuthbert or anyone else for that matter on board. And with all due respect your Alderton is hardly the sharpest tool in the box."

"Be that as it may, sir" said Nagle, "but he is most insistent _____."

"Just a second," interrupted Wallace, "Alderton had more alcohol than blood in his veins and in actual fact he spent most of that fateful evening coming and going. To the toilet, he claimed but who knows?"

"What are you suggesting, sir?"

"I'm not suggesting anything. It's just that your source is hardly a reliable witness given his frequent absences. There was also the issue that the two men had a falling-out in the recent past _____."

"Who?"

"Superintendent Hunter and Alderton, of course."

"Do you know what their falling-out was about?"

"No idea but I think Superintendent Hunter felt obliged to complain Alderton to his superiors. I know he felt a little guilty about that. But he was a very principled man."

"If you say so, sir. Now, you're saying with absolute conviction that there was no Mr. Cuthbert on board?"

"Absolutely. What is this all about anyway? It's obvious that it was an accidental drowning or are you suggesting that somebody was holding a grudge and deliberately pushed the poor man overboard? Dear, oh dear, that never even occurred to me. Have you spoken to the others?"

"Can you be specific about the time of the incident, sir?" Nagle asked, ignoring the question.

"Ah, you have me there. It wasn't only Alderton who had over-indulged. Perhaps we were all the worse for wear. I'm going to say around 10 o' clock. Or maybe closer to 11. Anyway, there or thereabouts."

"And where were you all immediately before the Superintendent went overboard?"

"Oh, we were just sitting around having an after dinner drink, enjoying the chat."

"And who was there?"

"Oh, just the three of us. As I said your Alderton was off somewhere. Claimed he was feeling sick."

"And then what happened?"

"Well, as you know, the sea was quite rough and suddenly a wicked wind whipped up so we scrambled to get as much of the stuff, glasses and bottles and that, below deck before everything took off."

"Hold on a minute," said Morecamb. "We were told that the sea was quite calm."

"By your trusty source?" smirked Wallace. "No, trust me, as a sea-faring man I can tell you that it was quite rough. Do you sail yourself, Morecamb?"

"Can you continue, sir?" interrupted Nagle who didn't show the least bit of intimidation. Or respect for that matter. "Let's stay on point, if you don't mind."

"Yes, well, as I said the weather suddenly deteriorated _____."

"How suddenly, sir?"

"Quite quickly, actually. So, as I say we decided to decamp. Grabbed as much as we could, you know, anything we could salvage. Anything that was in danger of being blown overboard."

"In hindsight, perhaps you should have grabbed Superintendent Hunter," murmured Nagle.

Wallace didn't deign to answer that but shifted his attention to Morecamb.

"Finished?" he asked.

"Can you get on with your story, sir?" said Morecamb, placing emphasis on the word 'story'.

"Right, so there we were, complete mayhem, glasses smashing all over the deck, the lights flickering off and on and the sea raging on all sides of us….felt as if we were under attack. And in the middle of it all I thought I heard Inspector Lonergan shouting my name _____."

"Over all the din and mayhem, sir?"

"Well I think I sensed it more than anything. You don't get to my rank without being acutely aware of atmosphere and an in-built sense of impending danger. A special radar, if you like."

"Sir," said Nagle sounding completely underwhelmed, "what happened then?"

"Well, I noticed Inspector Lonergan was gesticulating wildly and pointing frantically towards the sea. It was then I noticed that Superintendent Hunter was nowhere in sight so we both rushed to the railing and, as I said in my statement, called out his name until we were hoarse. Eventually we realised that there was no hope so we sent up flares _____."

"We've had no reports of any sightings of flares, sir."

"Well, have you met the lot in Kinsale?" snapped Wallace.

"So, you sent up flares and then what?"

"Well, when there was no response we headed back to shore."

"What time would this have been, sir?"

"Well, I can't say for definite. You must understand that we were traumatised at this stage _____."

"And drunk," added Morecamb. "Were there any witnesses when you docked?"

"None. I was expecting at least some of the local fishermen, on the assumption that they had seen the flares _____."

"Nobody saw the flares, sir."

"Yes, so you say but I find that hard to believe. In fact I don't believe it."

"Are you saying people are lying, sir?

"Well, let's just say there is a high incidence of alcoholism in those parts, I've been told. Quite the problem, I believe."

"Can we quote you on that, Superintendent?" asked Morecamb. "Maybe it's time the authorities in the relevant Government departments were alerted. We can't have an entire population in such close proximity to the Irish Sea wobbling around the place day and night putting themselves and everybody else in danger. Make a note of that, will you, Detective Nagle," Morecamb urged.

Wallace looked ready to explode.

"And what about Sergeant Alderton, sir?" continued Nagle.

"What about him? We searched for him, obviously, but couldn't see him. Maybe we should have searched more thoroughly but in view of what had happened we weren't thinking too clearly."

"And did it not occur to you that Sergeant Alderton might have suffered the same fate as Superintendent Hunter?"

"Well…fleetingly, maybe. But as I said he wasn't in our company immediately before the event occurred. So we just assumed that he was below deck somewhere."

"Right", said Morecamb, "thank you for your co-operation."

"No bother", said Wallace. "Glad to be of help. We're all just doing our bit to wrap this whole thing up and move on. Of course it will haunt me but I'm satisfied that we did all we could."

Wallace was a lot more relaxed now and seemed eager to show his magnanimity, even offering them refreshments and perhaps something small to eat.

"No, thank you. We're going to have lunch in the Shelbourne before we head all the way back to Cork. We had a lovely breakfast there before coming here."

"The Shelbourne?" Wallace asked and his eyebrows almost reached the top of his head.

CHAPTER 17

Nagle waited in the reception area of the station while Morecamb made his way up to the next floor where he knew the higher ranks hung out. An officer pointed him in the direction of O' Toole's office but as he neared it the great man emerged. He did a double take when he saw Morecamb but recovered immediately.

"Ah, Morecamb, good to see you. Come on in. I have a meeting but it can wait. So, you've spoken to Superintendent Wallace I gather. I trust everything is satisfactory? Full and frank disclosure, as they say. We're very eager to have all this business wrapped up. But I think it's fairly straight forward, is it not?"

"Not", said Morecamb.

"I don't follow. Would you care to explain?"

"Oh, Superintendent Wallace's tale was quite impressive, I'll grant you that. But we're sort of working in the dark a little _____."

"Who's working in the dark?" boomed a voice behind him. O'Toole hadn't fully closed his door obviously and was like a rabbit caught in headlights as the figure came further into the room. "Morecamb, what are you doing here? God, it's been years," said the newcomer and as Morecamb stood to greet his old friend he was immediately engulfed in a bear hug.

"Pete Drummond! My God, it's good to see you. Didn't realise you were back. Have you been promoted or demoted? Or fired, maybe?"

"Ever the optimist, Morecamb. Garda Commissioner, actually, for my sins. My God, it's great to see you."

"Em….. Commissioner," piped O'Toole, "the meeting? We probably shouldn't be late. We're meeting the Minister," he said with a definite hint of smugness in Morecamb's direction.

"Right, right," snapped Drummond and O' Toole retreated like a wounded dog. "Jim, I believe you're heading up the investigation into Hunter. How's that going?"

"Well, it would be going a lot better if we had access to a few vital documents."

"Oh?" said Drummond as he looked at O'Toole. "What's this all about?"

"Well, you see, there was a bit of a mix-up in Kinsale and some difficulty getting a suitable forensic team and em…."

"Get to the point, O' Toole."

"Well, we had to send our own team of forensics and then of course there was a delay in locating the body and all that……"

"What he's saying, Commissioner, is that we haven't been given access to the pathology report or forensics. All that information is here in Headquarters, under lock and key, hence, my reference to working in the dark."

"What the hell is going on, O' Toole?" shouted Drummond. "Who authorised this?"

"Well, you see _____."

"No. I don't see at all. This is damned unorthodox. I'm charging you personally with getting that information to our colleagues in Cork. Jim, you'll have it by tomorrow. Contact me as soon as you have them."

O'Toole looked as if he was sucking a lemon.

"Of course, sir," he mumbled.

"Right, that's sorted and Jim, I'll be down your way the week after next. We can catch up, have a few beers. I have your home number, I think. That's still the same or have you moved to more salubrious surroundings?"

"No, Pete, still roughing it. Looking forward to catching up."

"Good. Come on, O' Toole, let's see if the Minister knows what day of the week it is. You take care, Jim. We'll stay in touch."

CHAPTER 18

"So, Gwen.....I may call you 'Gwen', yes?" Without waiting for a response, McClean carried on. "Is there a significant other in your life?"

Gwen looked at him as if he'd sprouted horns. *A significant other? Who talks like that!*

"What do you mean?" she asked, playing for time.

"I mean, are you promised to somebody? You know, betrothed, in a monogamous relationship.....one of those. Anything?"

"Not that it's any of your business, but no."

They were on their way back to the station, very slowly. On Morecamb's instructions they had interviewed one of the fishermen who seemed to be one of the first responders on that fateful night in Kinsale.

That is to say he was one of the first to abandon his pint in the local hostelry and had ambled outside to see what all the commotion was about. So, strictly speaking, not one of the first on the scene but, according to himself, the most professional.

McClean had filled several pages in his jotter transcribing every utterance of their witness in spite of the glaringly obvious fact that their fisherman was making it up as he went along.

"We're both free spirits then," said McClean. "I would have thought that there would be someone special. You know, you're not bad looking."

He beamed at her feeling that he had given her a compliment, though nothing too effusive. His mother had warned him about giving women notions about themselves.

"Very kind of you," snapped Gwen.

"Not at all. So, what brings you Leeside?"

There he goes again. Why not say, 'Cork', like a normal person?

"Oh, just a change of scene, really," she said as casually as she could. "What about you?"

"Oh, Cork born and bred. We Cork people don't see any reason to move. We call it the 'real' capital."

"No," said Gwen, "that would be Dublin."

"Ever hear of Garretstown?" he asked as if she hadn't spoken. "Probably not. Well, it's a little sea-side hamlet on the outskirts of Kinsale and the family has a holiday home there. Spent many happy summers there as a child. Lots of the better Cork families have a pad down there. Can't divulge their names, I'm afraid. If I did I'd have to shoot you. That's a little joke by the way."

No harm in clarifying that, he mused. Women were notoriously prickly.

"Yes, I've heard Kinsale mentioned," Gwen said. "You were involved in quite a messy case down there last year, I believe."

"Right."

There was silence for a while after that and McClean might well have increased his speed a little. But it was only a temporary hiatus.

"This is one of our more famous landmarks," he announced with an extravagant sweep of his arm. "Blackrock Castle."

Gwen glanced to her left. It really was quite beautiful, majestic even, in the mid-day sunshine. Daringly perched on the edge of the river Lee, almost defying gravity. It had a large circular tower with jagged, tooth-like ramparts. Gwen had studied Art in school and had been fascinated in the Architectural module on the course. She had, briefly, even toyed with the idea of studying Art but her parents had threatened to disown her and throw her out of the house. So, going to college wasn't an option.

On the inland side of the Castle there was a huge cylinder tower rising several feet above the main structure.

"Is it open to visitors?" Gwen asked.

"I'm not sure," said her companion, "but I can find out. I'm free on Saturday. Would that suit you?"

Oh my God, thought Gwen, have I just initiated a date with McClean!

*****

It was quite the lunch.

Morecamb and Nagle sat back, replete, and lazily supped their pints. They had deliberately avoided any discussion about their recent encounter with Wallace and O' Toole. Time enough for that on the return journey to Cork. So they talked about family and house searches.

"Things are a lot pricier down here than I had imagined," said Nagle. "At the moment we're staying with the wife's people but it's a little cramped."

"How many children have you got?"

"Four but the wife would like one or two more. Frankly I wanted to stop after the first. Do you have children yourself?"

"God, no. I wouldn't know what to do with them. They're demanding little shits, I believe?"

"Oh, yes but you learn as you go along. And then, I believe, just when you think you have it all figured out they bugger off."

"Still, imagine what you would do if they didn't fly the nest, you know, refused to move out? It isn't as if you could have them forcibly removed....or could you? You know, like we do with the criminals. Unless of course they turned to crime," said Morecamb, staring off into the distance, wondering if he was cheering up his detective or driving him to the edge. But Nagle threw back his head and roared laughing.

"I'll have a word with the wife tonight," he said. "Something like that might change her mind about increasing our clutch."

Later, on the train, they exchanged views about the reason for their trip. They had managed to grab the last two remaining seats and were now enjoying another pint.

"What are your thoughts after today, Liam?" asked Morecamb.

"Interesting, to say the least. Wallace is a pup. We practically had to drag the information out of him and I bet we only got the half of it. But at least we got a more detailed account from him. What about you? You hinted that you were quite pleased with your encounter with O' Toole."

"Oh, not with O' Toole," and he went on to tell Nagle about Drummond. "We'll have those reports by tomorrow, he said and I believe him. But I'm a bit worried about Alderton, if I'm honest."

"In what way?"

"Well, a lot depends on the autopsy report of course. But if there's anything suspicious about Hunter's drowning then, it seems to me, that Alderton is on very shaky ground."

"I can see that. He's the only one who is unaccounted for on the night. At least nobody seems willing to give him an alibi."

"He's an outsider, isn't he," agreed Morecamb. "I mean there's nothing unusual in that. But he claims to have no knowledge whatsoever about the night, apart from bleating on about this Cuthbert man which doesn't help his cause. I mean he's never been the most reliable but, my God, are we to believe that he has gone completely ga-ga?"

"So, do you think that he just imagined this other man?"

"I doubt it but it's bloody typical of Alderton. He'd confuse a saint. Drunk or sober I don't think he's playing with the full deck. Don't know how he managed to get promoted to Superintendent. Might have used blackmail. We'll have to grill him again and advise him to get a solicitor. Anyway, drink up and we'll have another."

CHAPTER 19

There was only Nagle in the canteen the following morning when Gwen went in to snatch a cup of coffee. She had tossed and turned all night and it had been a relief to see the pink fingers of dawn trickling through her curtains.

"Any news, Gwen?"

"Oh God, yes!" she groaned. "I think I have a date with McClean on Saturday."

"Well," Nagle hesitated, "I was thinking more about the case. But, I must admit this sounds a lot more interesting. Did he use coercion? He doesn't carry a gun, does he?"

"Not as far as I know. But the problem is that I may have inadvertently given him the idea." She went on to tell him about her blunder. "I'm hoping he'll have forgotten all about it," she finished.

"Oh, I doubt that," said Nagle. "He'll have written it down in that little jotter of his and it wouldn't surprise me at all if he gets down on one knee and proposes," laughed Nagle.

"Right," snapped Gwen, picking up her coffee and marching towards the exit, "you've been a great help, Detective."

As the two of them pushed through the doors of the main incident room McClean, who was at the front of the room, jumped up and beckoned Gwen to the vacant seat beside him.

"Aw, isn't that lovely," murmured Nagle, sotto voce.

Morecamb was at the top of the room in front of the whiteboard and Thornhill was a little off to the side. Nagle noticed that two more officers were present, the extra staff promised by Thornhill, no doubt. Nagle still hadn't figured her out. She certainly seemed efficient and was very hands-on in the investigation. But, as he'd said to his wife the previous night, after he'd filled her in on the advantages of rearing criminals, Thornhill would be a good ally but a very able adversary. He wondered how long it would take before herself and Morecamb crossed swords. And he wouldn't like to bet on the outcome.

"Okay, everybody," called Morecamb. "House-keeping first. We have two extra officers joining our team today, thanks to Superintendent Thornhill. Care to introduce yourselves, gents?"

"Garda Lewis, sir."

"Garda Sullivan, sir."

"Good. You're welcome. Now, let's share our experiences from yesterday. Gwen? McClean?"

"Allow me, Gwen." McClean was up like a rabbit. Gwen shrank down into her chair in a desperate attempt to disappear. She just knew that Nagle would have a big grin on his face and, once again, cursed her earlier indiscretion.

"Well, Sergeant Cassidy and I had a most fruitful day." Here he paused.

Please don't wink at me, Gwen pleaded silently.

He did.

Gwen stole a glance at Morecamb who was frowning and scowling at the pair of them.

"So, to continue without further ado we interviewed one Slasher O' Donoghue, real name, Timothy. 5'10" in height, very much overweight and I would hazard a guess here _____."

"Don't!" barked Morecamb. "Facts only."

"Of course, sir. Well, in that case I can skip the first three pages of my notes. I personally felt it would be wise to write down every detail in the event _____."

"Continue."

"Okay, well, it was a little disconcerting to hear that he had spent the entire day leading up to the tragic event in the pub. Which brings me back to the weight issue......."

"I'm going to have to trash you, McClean, if you don't get on with it."

"Of course," squeaked McClean. "Anyway, to contextualise our interrogation yesterday, it seemed to me, and you, Gwen, that Slasher was a little intoxicated _____."

"He was practically comatose", snapped Gwen.

"Well, there I have to differ with you, Gwen, though I'm not for a moment _____."

"He was lying across a bench in the pub, sir, having spent the night there."

"That's true," agreed McClean, "but I still feel that we may have gleaned some nuggets of information _____."

"You have two minutes, McClean or else I'm going to make you clean the toilets", Morecamb interjected.

"Right," McCean acknowledged meekly, "so I'll just skip these few pages. Suffice to say that I'll put them on file for future reference. Right, chapter 4. Now this is interesting _____."

"Sit down, please, McClean, before I put you through the window. Gwen, the abbreviated version please," said Morecamb as he started to pace across the top of the room.

"Well, there isn't much to tell, sir." There was a sharp intake of breath beside her and she tried to ignore the frantic rustling of paper. She was also aware that McClean had raised his hand in the air.

"Slasher was drunk yesterday," Gwen continued, "and he was drunk on the night in question. There was a lot of jeering and yahooing from his yobbo friends in the bar while we were talking to him and trying to get some sense out of him. They seemed highly amused that we had chosen O'Donoghue as a possible witness. One of them even said that he hadn't been sober since 1961. The barmaid was a far better source of information _____."

"She was practically unintelligible," said McClean, "and very unsuitably attired, I might add."

"Unintelligible?" queried Morecamb. "Please don't tell me she was drunk as well."

"Oh, shut up, McClean", said Gwen. "She is a country girl, sir but I could understand her perfectly. So she told us that, as she was on her way to work on the morning of August the 12th she walked along by the quay where the boats are moored. She waved to Hunter and his friends who were preparing to set sail. She said they're regulars in Kinsale and often pop into the pub for a drink when they're down. Anyway, she distinctly heard one of them call to her in a very English accent, roaring, "All right, my lovely?"

"Rubbish," intoned McClean. "You should have seen the state of her, sir. Safety pins all over her attire and rings and pieces of metal hanging off her face. She reminded me of a wild boar and there is no way that men of Superintendent Hunter's status would even look at an apparition like that, much less salute her."

Morecamb ignored him. "Did she say how many were on board, Gwen?"

"She thinks about four, sir but admitted there may have been others below deck. But she was adamant that there was an Englishman on board."

"I think she was just confused, sir. She just assumed that anyone who spoke with a nice accent had to be a foreigner," offered McClean.

"And I think she sounds like a reliable witness," said Morecamb. "Did she give a description of the man?"

"No, she did not," puffed McClean.

"And whose fault is that!" roared Gwen. "You didn't give her a chance. You told her to be off about her business when she offered to sketch a likeness for us."

"McClean, as soon as this meeting is over I want you to go back down to Kinsale and bring that girl back here." "Gwen", continued Morecamb,

"I do apologise but you'll have to accompany him. And, McClean, leave that jotter of yours behind. Also, did you two get any chance to talk to Hunter's relatives?"

"No, sir," answered Gwen, glaring once again at McClean, "the journey to Kinsale and back took a lot longer than it should have."

"Right, well the priority is to get that bar assistant up here to do the sketches. I'll ask Moloney to ring ahead and let her know you are coming. You can talk to Hunter's relatives the first chance that you get after that. And remember what I said about that jotter, McClean."

Gwen didn't think she had ever felt so depressed in her life.

"Moving on, Detective Nagle and I paid a visit to our Masters yesterday." He went on to tell them about their interactions with Wallace and O' Toole and their stone-walling tactics.

"Thankfully we struck gold when we accidentally bumped into Garda Commissioner Drummond who promised to expedite the delivery of the Scene of Crime reports and the Pathology reports. I imagine we'll get delivery of those today and then, at least, we'll have something concrete. I intend getting Superintendent Wallace down here to get a more detailed statement, under caution, early next week.

Detective Nagle, will you get onto Store Street again and find out the status of those reports. Gwen and McClean, you already have your instructions." Then he turned to Thornhill whose look of horror was still trained on McClean, ever since he had first started to speak.

"Ma'am, could I have a word, please?"

"Certainly. That's probably a very good idea."

As soon as the door closed behind them Thornhill turned to him.

"Who is he?"

Morecamb was baffled.

"Where did he come from and why is he even on our team? And what's with the ridiculous way that he talks?"

"Ah, you mean McClean. Well, we think he may have crawled out from under some stone on the Bandon road _____."

"I'm serious. The man is a hindrance. He seems to barge into every situation with pre-conceived notions and refusing to allow that girl to sketch a likeness of this Englishman is a serious dereliction of duty. You will have to side-line him."

"I suppose I should but sometimes he accidentally can stumble across something relevant. Once he has somebody sensible and reliable with him he won't come to much harm. Besides, I couldn't send Gwen on her own".

"Well, you now have two extra Gardai at your disposal so use them. Anyway, what did you want to talk to me about?"

"It's about Alderton, Ma'am." Morecamb noticed that Thornhill's head snapped up at the mention of her predecessor and her mouth drew into a rigid line, almost obliterating her lips. The man is like a virus, he thought. Thornhill was barely in the door and already the mere mention of Alderton's name was a source of dissension.

"If the drowning turns out to be suspicious then Alderton is out on a limb. He has no alibi."

"But nobody is suggesting there was anything suspicious about it. I suggest we wait until we have the reports or were you intent on arresting him immediately, throwing the book at him, a very slight book I may add, and closing down the investigation."

Morecamb was stunned for a few minutes.

"Not at all, Ma'am," he bristled, "I'm simply stating the facts."

"But we don't have any facts, do we? And until we do I suggest you keep an open mind. Close the door on your way out."

For a moment they both eye-balled each other, then Morecamb turned on his heel and left.

CHAPTER 20

There was silence in the car as McClean drove at a sedate pace along the winding roads to Kinsale. Gwen didn't mind and focussed on the scenery.

It was a beautiful day. She had never believed Corkonians when they had waxed lyrical about their Mediterranean climate but since she had arrived they had been blessed with great weather though she would never admit it and certainly not to the twat at the wheel.

Every old man they met on the road saluted them, as if they were bosom pals. One or two were driving heads of cattle, no doubt moving them on to newer pastures. Both man and beast ambled along, the cattle flicking their tails from side to side in an effort to dislodge the flies which seemed to be a constant torment. The men carried a stick, probably hawthorn, but it seemed largely redundant and probably served as a walking aid rather than a weapon.

McClean spent his time muttering curses whenever they were forced to stop or slow down and seemed oblivious to the scenery – the dips and hollows on the road, the sycamore and ash swaying gently, the most spectacular rhododendrons vying for supremacy amongst the cornucopia of woodbine, clematis and those beautiful discreet primroses.

Through the open window Gwen could hear the thrum of farm machinery in the distance. Occasionally the blueness of the sky seemed to darken as a large scattering of crows swooped towards the ground, obviously in search of fallen grain. Harvesting time, then, she mused and imagined the excitement amongst adults and children alike as the contractor's combine harvester rolled and rumbled through gaps which had been hurriedly widened to accommodate the hungry monster.

The skies would have been studied minutely over the previous few days for any hint of rain, forecasters would have been cursed at, rosaries said. They knew that the first drop of rain would have signalled the abandonment of the harvest and the truculent contractor wouldn't be seen for days. And somehow there was always the hint that it was the farmer's own fault that it had rained.

But for today all seemed well with the world.

In no time at all, or so it seemed to Gwen, they were pulling up outside the pub in Kinsale.

"You're late", said a voice as the back door of the squad car was wrenched open and a waft of perfume and mad hair catapulted into the back seat. "You said you'd be here at two."

"I'm fairly sure you were told that was an approximation, Miss," snapped McClean.

"Melissa. That's my name."

McClean looked across at Gwen and rolled his eyes.

"Sorry, Melissa" said Gwen, "we were at a meeting and it ran late. How are you?"

For the next few miles the two women chatted amicably. Melissa was an entertaining and informative travelling companion. There was no mention of the case, just general chit-chat. McClean didn't join in and tried to ignore the raucous laughter in the back seat. Imagine Gwen partaking in all this nonsense and drivel.

"I think I may have to cancel our rendezvous on Saturday, Sergeant Cassidy", McLean blurted out. "It doesn't suit me on that particular day."

He didn't add that his mother had told him to 'play hard to get'. There was no doubt that the strategy had been a resounding success so far as he couldn't remember the last time he'd had a girlfriend.

"What did you have planned?" asked Melissa from the back seat, eyes round with curiosity.

"Nothing much," smiled Gwen, unable to help herself.

However, McClean could see she was putting on a brave face and was obviously gutted underneath. It was the smile that gave her away.

"If you must know, I was going to introduce Sergeant Cassidy to the delights of Blackrock Castle."

"Ooh, ace!" cooed Melissa, "that was where I lost my virginity, actually."

Gwen wondered which part of the structure lent itself to such activity. McClean wondered if he should reconsider his cancelled rendezvous with Gwen.

*****

Garda Lewis was hesitant as he approached Morecamb's door. He had noticed the thunderous scowl on his face as he had left Thornhill's office and wasn't relishing the prospect of the upcoming exchange. He tapped gently on the door and when there was no response he hesitantly entered, saw Morecamb was on the phone, hurriedly dropped the Scene of Crime report on the desk and almost fell out the door.

He reckoned the canteen was probably the furthest away so he made a bee-line for it. Nagle was occupying a table in the far corner so, as soon as he had loaded up his tray, he joined him.

"Alright, Lewis?"

"Yes, sir. Just dropped the SOC report to Detective Inspector Morecamb."

"Oh, good. What did he say?"

"Well, nothing really. He was on a phone call so I just left them on his desk."

"And now you're hiding, aren't you?" laughed Nagle.

"Pretty much, sir".

"Well, we'll know soon enough. If it's good news he'll come barging through that door and if it's bad news he'll come barging through that door. So, win-win or lose-lose, depends on your outlook."

Sure enough, ten minutes later, Morecamb barged into the canteen.

"What's all this then, Lewis?" he asked as he slapped the brown folder onto the formica-topped table. "An inventory of glasses, empty bottles, a few grainy photos of above and below deck, a number of upended chairs and an X marking the spot where Hunter bade farewell to the world."

"Lewis didn't compile the report, Jim," Nagle put in.

"And what if these are the only scene of crime photos?" Lewis asked, gaining courage from the support of the detective by his side. "Oh, and there's also a little note attached to the back of one of them from Commissioner O' Toole pointing out that as there is nothing whatsoever incriminating to be gleaned from the report he expects a speedy conclusion to the matter."

"Bloody cheek! Telling me how to do my job. Get us a cup of tea there, Lewis, like a good chap."

"Any sign of the Pathology report, Jim?"

"Well, if it's anything like this rubbish we needn't bother taking it out of the envelope."

"Why don't you get back onto your friend, Drummond and let him know?"

"That's all very well," said Morecamb, "but what can I say? I can't say we didn't get the report because we did and I can't say it's inconclusive because I don't know if it is or it isn't. Thanks, Lewis, put it down there. I bet Wallace is having a good laugh in his eyrie up in Dublin. I'll sort him out when he's on our patch. I just need something to throw at him but if I present this I'll just embarrass myself. Lewis, who delivered this?"

"I think it came by courier, sir. Sergeant Moloney called me down and gave it to me."

"And there was nothing else? No mention of a Pathology Report?"

"Well, he didn't mention anything else."

"Okay, I'll give Jane a ring and see if she got anything."

When Morecamb got through to the mortuary he was informed that Jane had gone home sick and no, her assistant didn't know anything about any reports 'languishing in her in-tray.' There followed a stand-off between the two men, Morecamb insisting that the assistant should tod-dle off to Jane's office and check.

No, he wouldn't be doing that, he wouldn't dream of breeching pro-tocol and if the Inspector wanted to pursue the matter further he could take it up with Miss Foley. However, did it not occur to him that Ms. Foley would have immediately contacted him if such material had been forwarded?

What a waste of space, thought Morecamb, and now Jane would blame the meat casserole from last night for her sudden illness and he would be getting it in the neck as soon as he went through the front door.

He re-joined Nagle and Lewis who were still in the canteen.

"Any luck?" asked Nagle though he could tell from the look on More-camb's face that it had been a spectacular failure.

"Nope. The Pathologist is gone home sick and her assistant is a twat with a Moussilini complex. Nagle, will you get on to Wallace's secretary and make an appointment for him to come down here, say tomorrow?"

As Nagle was on the point of getting up the door practically flew off its hinges and in trooped McClean followed by Gwen and a most spec-tacular looking young woman full of energy and attitude.

When Gwen spotted Morecamb she detoured over with her charge and introduced Melissa to her boss and colleagues.

"It isn't what I expected", said Melissa. "I thought there would be guns and high-powered men in dazzling uniforms with medals and things. But ye are all just very ordinary, aren't ye?"

"I'm afraid so, Melissa", laughed Morecamb. "But we try. I believe you're a bit of an artist?"

"Well, I dabble, in my spare time. But I'm good at likenesses. I enjoy studying faces."

"Good, that's what we need. Gwen, will you see that Melissa has a bite to eat and I'll get Alderton up to one of the interview rooms. Where's McClean gone?"

"Over there, sir," said Gwen, pointing to the furthest corner of the room. "Said he can feel a migraine coming on and wants a bit of peace and quiet."

"Right, I'm off to round up Alderton. You can sit here in my place, Melissa."

Morecamb didn't relish another battle with Alderton and God only knew what nonsense Murphy might start spouting. But when he opened the door the place was in darkness but through the gloom he could discern the unmistakable bulk of Murphy sprawled out in an armchair, fast asleep. With a smile he turned back towards the door and closed it with a mighty bang.

"What the _____.", spluttered Murphy.

"Working hard, Murphy, I see. Where's Alderton?"

"Gone to lunch and left me here on my own to look after the whole place. That's not fair, is it? The least I deserve is a promotion. If I'm considered responsible enough to man this place single-handedly then I think it's the least I deserve."

"Murphy, nobody believes you're responsible enough to man this place single-handed. Did Alderton say where he was going?"

"Nope. But I would think he's gone to lunch."

"Did he say when he'd be back?"

"Nope. Do you seriously think he would tell me stuff like that?"

"Well, he's certainly not in the canteen," said Morecamb as he opened the door to leave.

"Oh, I don't think the canteen would be posh enough for your Superintendent Thornhill."

"What?"

"The two of them went off together and Alderton was driving as they headed in the direction of town."

"What?"

*****

As Morecamb raged his way back to the canteen he knew he would have to find an escape valve for the many travesties in his life right now so he headed straight for McClean's table.

"What have I told you about this so called healthy eating of yours, McClean? It will kill you," he snarled as he brushed aside a banana skin and the core of an apple. "You can't possibly bring your best game to an investigation if……what are those shrivelled up things that you're stuffing into your mouth?"

"Sunflower seeds and raisins, sir. Would you like some?"

"Put them in the bin and come over to the other table to your colleagues, like any normal person."

As Morecamb headed back to the table Melissa started to get up but Morecamb motioned to her to stay where she was. When McClean was seated, still with the 'mouse-droppings' clutched in the little plastic bag, Morecamb turned to their guest.

"The man I wanted you to run your sketch by, Melissa, seems to have disappeared _____."

"Drowned?" she asked all wide-eyed and practically wobbling with excitement. "Cool!"

"I'm afraid not. But perhaps you could get started without him. I'm sure he won't be too long so Sergeant Cassidy will take you to one of the interview rooms. That okay. Gwen?"

"Yes, sir."

"Boss," said Nagle, having just returned from his effort to contact Wallace. "I could get no reply from Wallace's office. Maybe they're all on lunch. I can try _____."

"That's alright. McClean, you can do that. Ring the secretary and arrange that appointment with her boss, for tomorrow. Nagle, will you come with me?"

Morecamb led the way to his office and as soon as the door closed behind them he turned to his detective.

"I was just down with Murphy and it appears that Alderton and Thornhill have been seen heading off for lunch together. Mind you,

Murphy is the source and could well have imagined the whole thing but the fact remains that the two of them appear to be on the missing list at the same time. What do you make of that?"

"Is it possible that Alderton knew her in the past before she came here?"

"Then why would she come here if she knew him from before? In my experience, people usually head in the opposite direction. I can't bloody understand it. I mean, at the very least Alderton is linked to a possible crime scene and we now have the boss swanning off to lunch with him. What happens if we have to come down heavy on Alderton for any reason? Or indeed for no reason whatsoever? Say, for argument's sake, on a whim?"

"You need to be careful where you tread, Jim. We really need a few more hard facts before we ruffle any more feathers."

"Not my style, Liam. Not my style at all."

CHAPTER 21

McClean decided, on his way to make the phone call to Wallace's secretary, that it might be prudent to distance himself from any amorous attachment with Sergeant Cassidy. He was beginning to detect their incompatibility, based solely on gut instinct rather than anything approaching actual experience. Furthermore, he didn't want any distraction or impediment in the way of his imminent promotion, also based on gut instinct rather than actual experience.

Thus it was with a clean slate and a readiness to embark on a new, romantic journey that he found himself responding enthusiastically to the sultry and sexy voice of Sophia.....with an 'a', she breathed, and they spent the next thirty minutes, savouring the delights of their respective life stories.

It was so good to be conversing with a woman whose horizons stretched as far afield as Venice and Rome, who knew the difference between a Rose and a red wine and who didn't think that Wagner was a Polish car mechanic carrying out illegal repairs in a garage out in Bishopstown. He shuddered as he recalled that particular date.

Before finishing the call McClean had committed himself to driving all the way to Dublin on the first available weekend, buying her dinner, with wine, in a fancy restaurant and taking her shopping for clothes, and a handbag or two in Arnotts, followed by lunch.

He was still buzzing with excitement when he got back to the incident room and he suddenly realised that he'd forgotten the purpose of the phone call in the first place.....to ask Sophia to schedule the meeting between her boss and Morecamb.

When he hastily retraced his steps and tried to get through again the line was engaged. As he went back for the third attempt he bumped into Morecamb and Nagle coming against him.

"So, did you get through to the secretary, McClean?"

"Unfortunately, I've tried three times, sir, and the line is constantly engaged. I'm just on my way to have another go."

"Just leave it. I'll do it myself. You go along and see how Sergeant Cassidy and this Melissa girl are getting on with that likeness. Nagle, would you mind ringing Pathology again and see if you can get any further with that moron of an assistant."

Ten minutes later Morecamb had secured a promise from Wallace that he would 'grace' their premises the following afternoon. But this didn't alleviate the rage he was feeling towards McClean and the air in his office was blue with profanities when he realised that McClean had spoken to Wallace's secretary, hadn't mentioned anything about scheduling a meeting and, instead, had pestered her about securing a date. On his way to hunt him down he spotted Alderton and Thornhill on their return, at the other end of the corridor, outside the Super's office.

Alderton waved expansively when he spotted him and then gallantly opened Thornhill's door and ushered her inside. He was grinning like a cat as he approached Morecamb and made to go past him but an outstretched arm stopped him.

"Where do you think you're off to, Alderton? I've been looking for you and Murphy didn't know where you were."

"I don't furnish that clown with details of my itinerary. I find that the less interaction I have with him _____."

"Have you been drinking?"

"Just a glass or two of the old Boujoleau, for your information. I'd hardly debase the experience by calling it 'drinking', as you so crudely put it. And anyway, Caroline insisted. That's Superintendent Thornhill to you Morecamb and your boss, if you need reminding."

"And yours," snapped Morecamb. "Now get yourself along to Interview Room two. We've managed to secure the services of an artist who is going to do a sketch of this mystery man, maybe even with a bit of help from your good self."

"Boss," called Nagle as he came up behind him, "good news. That Pathology Report has arrived."

"Fantastic! Tell them to courier it over."

"Not the way it's done, old boy," smirked Alderton. "Someone from here will have to sign for it."

"What are you still doing here, Alderton? Clear off to that interview room."

"I'm afraid he's right, Jim," said Nagle as they watched the retreating figure of Alderton. "Miss Foley was quite insistent."

"Jane? Is she back then? I was told she had gone home."

"Obviously she's better. But she nearly took my head off when I suggested the courier business. Do you know her?"

"Yea. Girlfriend. But I never know from one day to the next. I'll go over and collect it now. And tell that McClean whelp if I see him before he sees me I'm going to give him the thrashing of his life."

*****

Alderton would be the first to admit that he did feel a little unsteady as he opened the door to Interview Room two but he backed out immediately when he spotted the strange creature with tattoos and enough iron on her face to be a source of envy to every blacksmith around. He was obviously in the wrong room so he tottered towards the next room along. As he neared his destination a woman's voice called him and beckoned him back.

"It's this room, Sergeant. We're in here."

The Sergeant of the female persuasion gestured to a chair in front of the so-called artist but Alderton ignored the pair of them and went over to sit beside the McClean chap who seemed to have distanced himself from the whole charade.

"What the blazes is going on over there?" he asked as he noisily dragged out a chair.

"Apparently our 'artist-in-residence' has the ability to solve the whole case at her fingertips," McClean said.

"Well, I hope they're not expecting me to engage with her," hiccupped Alderton. "The whole thing is completely unorthodox and I shall have a word with Caroline _____."

"Can you come over here, Sergeant Alderton, and take a look at these?"

Alderton grumbled his way across and fell into the vacant seat opposite the two women.

"What am I supposed to be looking at?" he asked as he squinted at an array of sketches spread out across the table.

"This is Melissa," began Cassidy.

"And I'm interested, why exactly?"

"She's a sketch artist and a very good one. And she's the only person who can verify if your Mr Cuthbert was on board with you on that fateful night."

"Well, I hardly need this person to corroborate what I know to be a fact."

"Just look at the drawings, Sergeant and tell me is there a likeness."

"Not a clue. They all look like cats and dogs to me."

"Perhaps if you turn them around, Sergeant, you might get a better view. There," snapped Gwen as she put the sketches the right way up. "By the way, do you normally wear reading glasses?" she asked as Alderton peered ever closer until his face almost touched the table.

"Nothing wrong with my eyesight. Anyway, my glasses are out in my car and I've no intention of going all the way back out to get them for this futile exercise." Then he stopped, picked up one of the sketches and held it at arms' length, squinting down the length of his nose.

"Could be…..I suppose….though I still think it resembles a monkey more than a human."

McClean sniggered in the corner and, in spite of her earlier confidence, Gwen could feel Melissa's embarrassment beside her.

"Well, we're back to where we started then," began Gwen.

"No surprise there," smiled Alderton as he began to leave.

"And you're the only person who claims this Cuthbert man was in the company OF A BUNCH OF DRUNKS," roared Gwen to the retreating bulk of Alderton as he slammed the door on his way out.

"They're very good sketches, Melissa but I think if Sergeant Alderton doesn't recognise this Cuthbert man in any of them then Cuthbert wasn't obviously in their company."

"But _____."

"Oh, I know you saw him on the deck. I believe you. But perhaps he was just helping out before they set sail."

"Shall I bin them?" asked McClean as he stopped by the table on his way out.

*****

It was with no small amount of trepidation that Morecamb locked his car and walked towards the Mortuary. Gingerly he knocked on Jane's door and somewhat reluctantly obeyed the shout to 'Enter.'

"I believe you weren't particularly nice to Jeremy earlier on the phone," was her opening salvo.

"Jeremy who?"

"My assistant pathologist," she replied, looking up at him beneath her eyebrows. "Some day you may be dealing exclusively with him as the pathologist and you ought to know that you should never, never antagonise the people you so desperately rely on."

Right, so where was all this going, Morecamb wondered. Was he being dumped or was she going to put in for a transfer? Possibly the States? She had been very taken with the States after all.

Gingerly, he began to lower himself into a chair.

"Actually, Jim, I think I may be pregnant."

Morecamb immediately catapulted out of the chair which crashed to the floor behind him.

An ashen-faced Jeremy poked his head around the door and asked if everything was ok. "It's just that I heard the noise....."

"No, Jeremy, everything is fine. Come on in. Detective Inspector Morecamb has something to say to you."

"I have?" queried Morecamb, sensing that he was rapidly losing control of the situation.

Jeremy backed up a little towards the door.

"Go on, Jim, apologise for your behaviour."

Morecamb turned back towards Jane still trying to grapple with her news.

"Well, I hardly think I'm the only one responsible here," he said. "You were always more than a willing participant."

"I wasn't even there," snapped Jane, "so you can hardly accuse me of anything."

Morecamb could feel the breath catch in his throat and in his confusion he wondered if it was Jeremy who had impregnated his girlfriend. But Jane had said she wasn't even there so did that mean he had spent a night with the wet sop cowering near the door. Idly he wondered if he was having a cardiac arrest.

"Apologise to Jeremy for the way you spoke to him earlier on the phone." She enunciated each word as if she was speaking to an idiot.

The relief brought beads of sweat out on Morecamb's forehead. *So that's what this was all about. Well, some of it anyway.*

"Of course. Oh, thank God," he breathed, his face creased in a big smile. "Sorry, Jeremy, I take full responsibility. I should not have spoken to you like that. I'll talk to you later tonight, Jane. Or maybe tomorrow. Depends on what time I get home," he added as he pushed Jeremy aside and reached for the door handle.

"Aren't you forgetting something, Jim?"

Morecamb looked at her blankly and wondered what was coming down the tracks now.

"The Pathology Report, you idiot."

"Oh, of course. Oh, thank God."

With the report grasped in his hand he scarpered through the door and headed out into the sunlight.

*****

He sat in the car for a long time trying to digest Jane's news. It certainly hadn't been part of the grand plan. But, then again, there had been no grand plan just a quiet determination, on Morecamb's part, to never get married again or have children.

Four years earlier his then wife, Fiona, had left him, for greener pastures she had informed him, and he no longer even wondered where she was now. In reality the marriage was dead in the water before she ever closed the front door behind her for the last time. Morecamb had tried not to allow the resultant bitterness to engulf him.

In those earlier halcyon days of their marriage there had been a grand plan; to grow old together having raised four children ...... two boys and two girls. But nothing had worked out.

Fiona had got pregnant alright and Morecamb could still remember his unbridled joy when she told him the news. My God, he was walking on air. He had been an only child and the thought of having his own brood was like a fanfare of kaleidoscopic colours during his every waking moment.

On the streets he took a newfound interest, indeed joy, as he passed by mothers pushing prams and buggies and often stole a quick glance at the swaddled bundle lurking snugly in the folds of a soft blanket. Was it a boy or a girl he would wonder? What age? Sometimes he'd played a game where he would guess the age of the child and then of course he would have to stop the mother to confirm if he was within a ballpark of the correct age.

When he had confided all this to Fiona she had ridiculed him and told him he could get arrested for harassment. So he had contented himself with just looking but every time he had marvelled at the miracle of it all.

One thing which had struck him quite forcibly during that time was the fact that men never seemed to be pushing the pram. Alright, they were obviously working during the day but what about in the evening? Well, he certainly envisaged playing a full role and he couldn't wait.

The only cloud on the horizon had been Fiona's muted response to her pregnancy and as the days wore on she became less and less communicative, more moody and eventually refused to have any discussion about the pregnancy.

Monday the 14th April is still embedded in his memory.

Fiona had been staying with an old school friend up in Dublin for the weekend. Morecamb had been glad for her as he felt that it might help to dispel some of her lethargy. He had done a lot of reading up on the subject of pregnancy and fancied himself a bit of an expert on hormones and mood swings and cravings.

Maybe, after the weekend away, she would be more willing to engage and share in the excitement. But as soon as she arrived home on the Sunday night she went straight to bed, in the spare room. Morecamb had spent the night tossing and turning and wished he didn't have to go into work the following morning. But, he was going to be a family man soon and any hesitancy about showing up for work was instantly dispelled. Besides, he had reached the decision that he would apply for a promotion. His family would have the very best.

Well, here he was now, a few years later, sitting in his car, a Detective Inspector. He had got his promotion and nobody cared, least of all himself.

Because Fiona had indeed met her friend on that weekend, flown to Birmingham and had the pregnancy terminated. She had informed him in cold, matter-of-fact terms. She wasn't ready for the responsibility. She was too young to be tied down. She wasn't even sure she would ever want to be a mother. There had been no apology. No remorse. No discussion.

Morecamb had left the house that Monday night, didn't turn up for work the following day or the next day and spent the rest of the week in a state of perpetual drunkenness. He'd never told anybody. Looking back he wondered if he'd admitted it even to himself. Ever afterwards he'd avoided looking at prams, buggies, pregnant women.

He never forgave Fiona. But it didn't seem to bother her and she'd resumed her social life as if she was single again.

Within six months she was, effectively, single again. There was a note on the kitchen table one evening when he'd come home from work. She was gone and wasn't coming back. Morecamb had read the message as if it was intended for somebody else, a stranger perhaps. And he felt like a stranger within himself. There were times when he was a stranger looking in at another stranger.

And, what now? What next? Slowly he turned on the ignition and eased his way out of the car park. He'd completely forgotten about the Report which he'd thrown onto the passenger seat.

Lewis seemed to be the sole occupant of the station when he got back and when he asked him about the others he was informed that Nagle had volunteered to give Melissa a lift back to Kinsale. Sergeant Cassidy had gone with them. Melissa had wanted to take a bus or hitch a lift as she refused to travel with McClean. Not that he had offered anyway. Oh, and McClean had received an urgent message from his mother, something to do with a doctor's appointment though that had only materialised after Nagle's dire warning that he should make himself scarce. Lewis didn't divulge that last bit to Morecamb.

After grabbing a quick cup of coffee Morecamb retreated to his office, pulled the blinds and snapped on the light. As soon as he started to read the report Jane's news was instantly forgotten. The whole case had just become a lot more complicated.

Quietly he sat there, mulling over the ramifications. He desperately needed to run it by Nagle but he probably wouldn't be back for another hour or two. And he couldn't go to Thornhill, at least not yet.

Suddenly he could feel a pounding headache crawling up the back of his neck and coiling itself around his forehead. It was way too early to go home so he locked the report in a drawer, grabbed his car keys and headed to the nearest pub.

At eleven o' clock he called a taxi and headed home.

All the lights in the house were off, never a good sign. So he crept into the sitting room, threw himself down on the sofa and was fast asleep within minutes.

CHAPTER 22

The following morning, through a painful haze, Morecamb remembered that he didn't have his car to get into work and when he heard the front door slam as Jane headed off to the mortuary he realised he would have to call another taxi. Slowly, he eased himself off the settee and gingerly put his feet on the floor, all the while holding onto his head with both hands.

As luck would have it wasn't it the same bloody taxi driver who had delivered him home the previous evening and who lost no time in telling him that he looked like a man who had slept in his suit, smelt like a brewery and who would benefit enormously from a pair of shades.

"Here, have these," he said as he tossed a pair of sunglasses at Morecamb.

"Some punter left them behind a few days ago. Drunk as a skunk and could barely get in and out of the car. No offence."

The first person he met when he went into the station was Alderton who seemed to be heading in the direction of Thornhill's door.

"Alderton," he called, "where are you going?"

"I've an important meeting with the Super."

"Well, it will have to wait. My meeting takes precedence."

"What meeting?"

"I'm about to call an important meeting with my team so clear off. But don't go far. I'll need to speak to you too so don't stir from the Cold Cases' Unit."

Then he spotted Gwen. "Sergeant, will you call everyone to the Incident Room, including the Superintendent? I'll be there in five minutes. I just want to get something in my office."

*****

Ten minutes later they were all assembled and Morecamb joined Thornhill at the top of the room.

"Okay," he called, "a quick recap. Sergeant Cassidy, how did Melissa get on yesterday? Any breakthrough?"

"I'm afraid not, sir. Sergeant Alderton didn't seem to think there was any resemblance between his Mr. Cuthbert and the sketches. He was actually quite disparaging."

"Well, maybe he'll try a little harder today when I've had a word with him. Where are the sketches now?"

"They're in my possession," said Thornhill, "and if Sergeant Alderton said there's no resemblance then we must take his word for it. We certainly don't want him to fabricate anything in order to suit somebody's agenda."

Morecamb turned away, ignoring her barbed contribution and faced his team again.

"Superintendent Wallace is due around two thirty. No thanks to you, McClean."

McClean had the good grace to look embarrassed.

"I also have the Pathology Report and it makes for interesting reading. The most relevant detail is the finding that Superintendent Hunter was dead before he ever hit the water. There was no water found in his lungs and there was a rather nasty bump on the side of his head, just above his left ear lobe. So he more or less had his skull crushed before being helped over the rails to his eternal peace and now we are looking at a murder enquiry."

You could hear a pin drop in the Incident Room. The first to break the silence was Gwen who emitted a loud sob and immediately left the room. Morecamb did wonder afterwards if it was a sob or a giggle. He would check it out.

McClean raised his hand and announced that he had shown amazing foresight when he had studiously copied each utterance of 'Slasher O Donovan', their sole witness. Nagle, who was sitting behind him, reached forward and tugged on his jacket, forcing him to resume his seat and whispering to him to shut up.

Thornhill hadn't uttered a word.

"Nagle, will you get on to Wallace's secretary and tell her to inform her boss that he'll need legal representation. I'm sure he will have organised that anyway but just in case. McClean, can I trust you to make copies of this report, without trying to organise a date with the photocopier, and give one to each of the team. Superintendent, could I have a word in private, please?"

There was a sudden burst of activity and he followed Thornhill out of the room, As they left Morecamb could hear McClean extolling, once again, the wonders of his own foresight in transcribing, verbatim, the words of their sole witness.

Thornhill stood ramrod straight behind her desk as Morecamb closed the door behind him and her gaze never wavered from his.

"Before you start I want to state that I have absolute confidence that Sergeant Alderton had nothing whatsoever to do with Hunter's death. It is simply not in his nature. I know that you two don't see eye to eye but I won't stand by and give you a carte blanche to exercise a vendetta against an honourable man."

"It is not a vendetta, Ma'am and I never once suggested that Alderton is our culprit. But the fact remains that he was on board when a man was murdered so we can't ignore that. And, at the very least, he is a person of interest. Probably for the first time in his life, I might add."

"And what about the other two on board? Wallace and Lonergan?"

"So, are we dismissing the other man that Alderton claims to have seen?"

"I think it would be best for the moment and concentrate on the obvious suspects."

"But not Alderton? Look, I want to put this as delicately as possible. Your relationship with Alderton _____."

"There is no relationship with Sergeant Alderton," she snapped.

"Well, whatever it is I suggest that it might be prudent to be a little more circumspect in your dealings with him."

"Inspector Morecamb, you would be well advised to remember that I am your superior and I have no intention of ostracising an innocent man on your say-so. And remember, innocent until proven guilty. Now I suggest that you get back to some real work."

'A flea in the ear' came to mind as Morecamb left Thornhill's office. Between Jane and Thornhill he felt ambushed, under attack. Which reminded him, he should speak to Gwen to remind her that she and McClean needed to get on to Hunter's crowd. Hopefully she was back in the Incident Room.

*****

It took a good ten minutes for the shaking to subside and when Gwen saw her reflection in the mirror in the bathroom she looked like someone who had been dragged through a ditch.

As soon as she had rushed out of the incident room she had locked herself in a toilet cubicle and fought to control her emotions. What the hell was wrong with her! She had been quite accepting, almost sanguine, when Hunter's death was deemed accidental. But murder was a whole other game.

And why now did images of the early days of their relationship have to surface? Why now was she remembering the little gifts he had showered on her? His considerate love-making? The furtive glances between the two of them when they happened to be in the same room? The gentle brush of his hand against hers in the corridor when nobody was looking. The almost childish glee when he smuggled her into his friend's apartment and the joy and indeed privilege when she cooked breakfast for him the following morning before they both set off, separately, to work, he in his car whilst she took the bus. She couldn't wait until it was all out in the open and they could travel together. And she was certain that he wanted that too.

As she struggled to restore some semblance of normality to her features she berated herself for her sentimentality. Why did it matter if his death was accidental or murder? But the image of that fatal blow caused the tears to flow again. Perhaps she should ask to go home. Plead sickness. But she didn't think Morecamb would be easy to hoodwink.

She splashed her face with some more water, patted it dry with some tissues and marched towards the incident room with as much confidence as she could muster. And God help whoever gave her grief.

"Gwen, Detective Inspector Morecamb was looking for you," McClean piped up. "We have to talk to the late Superintendent's distraught relatives as soon as possible so I suggest immediately. I've left a copy of the Pathology Report on your desk and I've also taken the liberty of photocopying the parts of the interview with Slasher which some people, yourself included, chose to ignore but I bet you're glad now that I had the foresight to _____."

McClean's words of wisdom came to an abrupt halt as Gwen snatched up the precious chapters, ripped them in half and tossed them in the bin. She gave the Pathology report a cursory glance before heading off into the canteen, ignoring the startled looks of McClean, Lewis and Sullivan.

CHAPTER 23

The following day, after a rushed lunch, Morecamb beckoned to Nagle and they adjourned to the Inspector's office to discuss strategy on the upcoming interview with Wallace. He had considered asking Thornhill to sit in on the meeting but he was slowly coming to the realisation that she was a bit of an enigma. It wasn't that he didn't trust her but he suspected that her support was, at times, less than wholehearted. He was tempted to confide in Nagle whom he liked and trusted but the fact remained that he was a relative newcomer to the team and it mightn't be fair to prejudice his opinion in any way.

"Right," began Morecamb, "I think we should adopt a charm offensive."

That certainly got Nagle's attention.

"You mean as distinct from beating him to a pulp?"

"Yes, something along those lines. Let him think that we believe everything he spews out. Be all sweetness and light. Give him a false sense of security and then hit him with the Pathology results. What do you think?"

"Sweetness and light……"

"Yes, we can afford to be magnanimous because let's face it we have the upper hand. You can let me lead. I wonder who his legal representative is."

When they entered the interview room it was to the sound of raucous laughter. Wallace seemed to be regaling his brief with some hilarious anecdote and took his time reaching the punchline, completely ignoring their arrival.

"We haven't got all day, gentlemen," said Morecamb as he and Nagle sat across from the two men. "This interview is being recorded so state your names clearly for the tape."

Both men obliged, McIntosh being a Senior Council with a very wide girth, courtesy no doubt, of too many free lunches and sporting perfectly manicured talons which suggested too much free time on his hands. Wallace was equally pristine beside him and for a brief moment Morecamb felt a little uncomfortable knowing that he and Nagle looked somewhat dishevelled in their presence. He was thrown for a moment and was silent. He was vaguely aware of his sergeant glancing at him and then he heard Nagle speaking.

"So, Superintendent Wallace, you assured us when we were in Dublin that you had given a full and frank statement of events in Kinsale and signed your name to that effect. Correct?"

"Absolutely."

"And just for the purposes of this interrogation _____."

"Meeting," snapped McIntosh.

"Murder," said Morecamb.

There was a stunned silence in the room as three heads swivelled in his direction. Of the three Nagle seemed the most confused.

"Yep," Morecamb continued. "Geoffrey Hunter was murdered."

"Fuck off," roared Wallace.

"Quite," said McIntosh.

"So, we're in a little pickle here or should I say, you are."

"Don't be ridiculous, you bloody fool _____."

"David, David, let's not rise to this scurrilous attempt to upset you. Leave this to me. Explain yourself, Morecamb."

"Inspector Morecamb, actually. And I thought I had been rather clear in my statement just now. What do you think, Detective Nagle?"

"Well, sir, perhaps you should flesh it out a bit and then we can process Superintendent Wallace's detention and be home on time for supper."

"Good idea. I'll keep it brief. Hunter was hit over the head with a blunt instrument and was well and truly dead before he was dispatched into the water."

"That's a lie," screamed Wallace. "He was alive before he went overboard."

"I thought you didn't see him going overboard so how do you know he was alive? That doesn't make sense to me. What about you, Detective?"

"Quite the mystery, I agree. But the Pathology Report certainly seems to back up your assertion, sir."

"We already saw the Pathology Report," said McIntosh, "and it most certainly does not support your scurrilous accusation."

"You saw a pathology report, obviously the sanitised one _____."

"Do you realise what you're saying here, Morecamb?"

"Do you, Mr. McIntosh? And the first thing we asked your client when we sat down was if he was happy with the statement he had given us and his answer was an emphatic yes."

"I'm not listening to anymore of this bullshit," said Wallace as he started to get up off his seat.

"See, that's where you're wrong, Superintendent. You'll leave the room when we say you can. Detective Nagle, will you do the honours and give us a brief summary of Superintendent Wallace's statement regarding the night of the tragedy."

Nagle rattled off the salient points of the statement while Wallace stared straight ahead and McIntosh inspected his nails. When he had finished McIntosh reached out and snatched the statement.

"I see absolutely nothing wrong with that statement," said McIntosh. "It's a true and accurate account of the events on that night and my client has signed his name to that."

"Indeed," said Morecamb, "and he has signed his name on several documents. He seems to have been most obliging. For example, he has signed off on the Scene of Crime Report as well and his name appears on each page of the actions which were taken that night. Let me see, he was the person who sanctioned a crew from his own jurisdiction in Dublin to carry out the initial inspection of the scene, sending the Cork lads home. The officers in Kinsale were pushed aside and told their duty was to keep the locals in the bar and prevent them from getting close to the scene. Then, at first light the following morning you were the person who arranged for the boat to be brought to Dun Laoighre harbour."

"Well, somebody had to take charge," said Wallace, his face a nasty shade of purple at this stage. "Those oafs in Kinsale don't know their arse from their elbow."

"I don't see Inspector Lonergan's dabs anywhere on any of the documents, just yours."

"No, he went on ahead to Dublin to look after things at that end".

"What things?"

"Well, obviously to report the incident to the Commissioner and other superior officers at H.Q."

"I need some time alone with my client," McIntosh interjected. "Shut that contraption off and give us some privacy. "

"By all means. You have 30 minutes max."

*****

"What do you think?" Nagle asked as they made their way to the canteen.

"Oh, I fully expect a 'no comment' for the rest of the afternoon. But perhaps McIntosh will see the benefit of some form of damage limitation. Should be interesting."

Just as they reached the door of the canteen Thornhill hailed them and asked for an update.

"Not much progress, Ma'am," answered Morecamb. "We just went through the statement which Wallace gave us in Dublin _____."

"I haven't seen that statement, have I? I'd appreciate if you could leave it on my desk as soon as possible."

"Well, we're going back to continue the interrogation of Wallace in thirty minutes _____."

"Any time before that will be fine," she replied as she headed back to her office.

Nagle raised his eyebrows but didn't make any comment. Neither did Morecamb.

*****

When they re-joined Wallace and his brief there was no hilarity in evidence this time.

Wallace had a more chastened and sombre demeanour and McIntosh was displaying renewed interest in his manicure.

Morecamb motioned to Nagle to turn on the tape recorder again and before either of them could speak McIntosh flapped his hand in the air and informed them that he would now read a short statement prepared by his 'honourable friend' and at its conclusion no further questions would be dignified with an answer.

The statement was succinct. Wallace denied all knowledge of any circumstance whereby his late friend, Superintendent Hunter, could have adversely met his end or indeed had been helped towards that eventuality. He could also attest with certainty that his friend, Lonergan, was a man of impeccable character and had been in his company at all times. On the other hand Superintendent Alderton's whereabouts for much of the journey were a mystery but, on reflection, he remembered there were times when the dear departed and Alderton had been 'in absentia' at the same time. And there was no Mr. Cuthbert.

"So, in other words, sir, you're basically sticking to your original statement?"

"No comment," said Wallace.

"Nagle, will you throw these two out, please? We'll be in touch, Superintendent Wallace. Don't leave your immediate locality."

"What? Not even to go sailing?" Wallace smirked.

CHAPTER 24

Morecamb stormed out of the room and headed towards the Cold Cases' Unit. For once both men were in situ and seemed to be doing some work.

"Alderton, can I have a word, please? Murphy, will you excuse us for a few minutes?"

"Well, I'm just in the middle of some rather important work, boss," said Murphy, giving him a huge wink which could be seen from outer space, "if you get my drift." Another wink. "And I'm anxious _____."

"Get out."

Both men waited until the door closed behind Murphy and then Alderton announced that he was writing out a letter of resignation for Murphy which he would be forced to sign on his return.

"Forget all that, Alderton. I'm here to give you a piece of friendly advice. Get yourself a lawyer. You're going to need one."

"What the blazes are you talking about, Morecamb?"

"Alderton, Hunter was murdered _____."

"Yes, I know, Caroline told me. In fact I probably knew before you did."

"No, Alderton, you didn't because I'm the person who told Superintendent Thornhill. Unless of course you were the person who murdered him and in that case, yes, you did know before I did."

"Don't be ridiculous! Why on earth would I do that?"

"Look, I'm doing you a favour here. We've just had Wallace in for questioning and it seems to me that he and possibly Lonergan are going to hang you out to dry."

"Always the drama queen, Morecamb."

"Both Wallace and Lonergan are going to give each other a rock solid alibi. You have no alibi for the time of Hunter's death and while I don't for a minute think you have the wit or the physicality to knock Hunter over the head and haul his sorry carcass overboard _____."

"How dare you! I'm as capable as the next man of murdering someone and disposing.........."

"On second thoughts, maybe a team of lawyers," said Morecamb as Alderton's declaration petered to a stop. "And throw in a few barristers for good measure."

*****

"He's an awful eejit," said Nagle when Morecamb told him about his interaction with Alderton.

"I know. I'm beginning to wonder if his proximity to Murphy is having a negative impact. I'm not saying that he was ever the sharpest tool in the box but at the moment he seems to be quite capable of walking voluntarily to the gallows, offering the rope to the nearest bystander and inviting them to hang him until his head falls off."

Moloney's head appeared around the door and announced there was a telephone call for Morecamb.

"I'll take it in my office. Put it through,"

When he opened the door to his office the place was in darkness and he almost collapsed when a silhouette unfurled itself from a chair and advanced towards him.

"Now, Boss, you know I'm a reasonable man _____."

"No, you're not, Murphy. And what the hell are you doing in my office?"

"I've come to report. And to complain _____."

He was interrupted by the ringing of the telephone and instead of clearing off like any sensible individual he sat back down and nonchalantly crossed his legs.

"Morecamb speaking."

"Ah, Jim, just ringing for an update and to make sure that you got all those documents that you asked for."

"Pete! Good to hear from you. Yes, we got all those documents. Thanks for that."

"So, how's it going?"

"Well, we just had Wallace and his Brief entertaining us. Didn't make much progress. He stuck to his original statement."

"And do you think there's any way you can get him to change that? I mean, do you think he could be complicit in any way in what went on?"

"Well, I don't trust him and as I said before both his statement and Lonergan's are almost identical and that alone makes me suspicious. And I can't help wondering about this Cuthbert man."

"Well, you said yourself that Alderton isn't the most reliable. Look, do you want me to have a word with Wallace or Lonergan?"

"No, no, that's okay. We'll handle it down here. It's landed on my desk so I'm determined to see it through. Anyway, when are you coming down for that pint? You're more than welcome to crash at my place."

A quick glance at Murphy revealed a look of consternation on his face and an emphatic shaking of his head.

"Well, I have to go away for a few days. Usual bureaucratic meetings but hopefully soon. And, who knows, this bloody business might be sorted by then and we can turn it into a celebration."

"Great, Pete. See you then. And thanks again."

"Who was that?" asked Murphy as Morecamb replaced the receiver.

"You wouldn't know him, Murphy. An old friend of mine. Pete Drummond. He's one of the top brass now. We trained together. Now, why were you shaking your head when I was inviting him to stay at my place?"

"Well, the last time I was in your house I was made to feel most unwelcome. In fact, if I recall correctly you threatened to shoot me. And your missus _____."

"Girlfriend."

"_____. wasn't exactly welcoming either. And I've known you far longer than she has so I think I'm entitled _____."

"Stop rambling. You said you had something to report so spit it out."

"Well, it's Alderton. He's been acting very suspiciously all morning. Constantly writing, page after page and then ripping them up and throwing them in the bin. I sneaked over at one stage, well, a few times, to see what he was writing and I swear to God he growled like a dog. He's not right in the head. And he was on the phone twice to Thornhill, whispering, and constantly looking over his shoulder at me."

Morecamb's interest piqued.

"Any idea what they were talking about?"

"Something about a sketch so I believe they were arranging to go to the Opera House or maybe The Everyman Theatre to see a play. Oh, and your name was mentioned a few times. You're not going with them, are you?"

For a second time Murphy was ordered out and told not to come back.

As soon as he was gone Morecamb decided he would go back to the pathology unit only this time he would bring Nagle with him. That should stave off any fireworks.

CHAPTER 25

"Okay, McClean, I'll talk Hunter's brother and sister and will you talk to his in-laws?" suggested Gwen. They were in the Incident Room and, as it was quiet, Gwen suggested they should take the opportunity to speak to the relatives of 'the dead man'.

"Actually, I think I should take his sister, though not literally you understand. Isabel, isn't it? Being a "young man about town'"…..fingers in the air…… "I feel that I might connect better with her. It has been my experience _____."

"Right," snapped Gwen, "just get on with it."

McClean rubbed his hands in glee. He was beginning to have doubts about Sophia, with an 'a', Wallace's secretary. Whilst he liked to spoil a girl, only on the first date, mind, he felt his tryst with Sophia might extend, inadvertently into a second day. After all she had mentioned a day of shopping following on from their dinner date and, tempting though it was, he felt that scrambled egg on toast would not justify the resultant shopping spree.

"Ah, may I speak with Miss Isabel Hunter, please?"

"Speaking."

"Well, first of all may I say what an honour and a privilege…….."

Gwen tuned out. Morecamb would have his guts if he knew the sycophantic nonsense being spewed at the other side of the desk. Time to get on with her own task and she decided to start with the parent-in-laws.

"May I speak with Mr. Bishop, please?"

"Who is this?"

Gwen introduced herself and she could hear a sharp intake of breath.

"I didn't realise that we had females......well, never mind. Carry on."

"Yes, we're investigating the circumstances into your son-in-law's murder _____."

"Pardon? Murder?"

"Yes," said Gwen, her brow beginning to furrow.

"First I've heard of it!"

"Well, we did suggest the possibility of it being a murder to your daughter. Did she not mention that to you?"

"Certainly not! Anyway she's abroad, taking a well-earned rest after all the nonsense around the man's funeral. So, you think he was murdered? Well, well."

There was a pause and then Gwen heard him call to somebody in the background, "Jennifer, the shitester was murdered. Shot, was he," addressing Gwen again, "or bludgeoned to death, maybe?"

"I'm afraid I can't discuss any of the details of an ongoing investigation. But, I was wondering, that is to say we were wondering if you know of anybody who might have held a grudge against the deceased?"

"You mean a list?"

"Well, em, something like that, yes."

"Jennifer!" Again the roar. "They want a list of Geoffrey's enemies."

There was a muffled reply and then he was back on the phone again. "My wife said she will fax it down to you. Anything else, Sergeant?"

"Well, perhaps you could tell me a little about your late son-in-law?"

"Not a lot to say, really. Well, no, that's a lie. There's plenty but I don't wish to speak ill of the dead. No, that's a lie too. Let's just say we were appalled when Olivia dragged him in. No class, you understand. Didn't even know how to use a knife and fork. Complete savage. Makes me shudder when I think about it. But she had her heart set on him so what could we do? Jennifer believes she was going through the rebellious teenage stage, at 25 I might add. Personally I felt she was having a mental break down."

"So," interrupted Gwen, "apart from his dubious table manners was there anything else?"

"Quite simply, he was a gold digger and a social climber. Saw an opportunity to swan around all the best establishments on my coat tails." The voice at the other end of the phone had risen several octaves. "He even joined the same golf and yachting clubs as myself and he without so much as a paddle. And of course his connection to this family was a huge advantage in climbing the ladder within the bloody Garda force."

"Yes, well none of that seems sufficient reason for his murder," said Gwen.

"I'll have you know, young lady, that any one of those is more than justification for his bloody murder."

"And where were you, Mr. Bishop on the 14th of August?"

"Well, I'll have to check my diary, won't I? I'm a very busy man."

"And what about your wife?"

"My wife?" he asked, incredulously. "Here, you can speak to her yourself. Jennifer, some whipper snapper wants to ask you some questions."

"Mrs Bishop," began Gwen, "I just want to ask you _____."

"Let me stop you there, dearie. It's Miss Lonergan. I retained my maiden name. Daddy didn't see why I should surrender my identity as well as a bloody great fortune to my future spouse, as well as my virginity but that's another story. Furthermore _____."

"Excuse me, Mrs Bish….. I mean Lonergan, are you by any chance related to Inspector Lonergan who was on board the vessel from which your son-in-law met his death?"

"Of course, Toby is my brother. I thought you said you were investigating the death of my son-in-law? You haven't got very far, have you?"

Gwen was flummoxed. How had that connection escaped them? And why didn't the bloody widow say anything?

"I believe you want to know where I was at the time of the unfortunate event? Well, I was at my Bridge club and Mr Bishop was at a Rotary meeting. Hello? Are you still there?"

"Yes", mumbled Gwen.

"See, I'm doing your job for you. You didn't even have to ask the question."

And with that the line went dead.

Gwen leaned back in her chair, rolled her eyes heavenwards and groaned out loud. God, there would be hell to pay and a long lecture from Morecamb, no doubt, on the sloppiness of the investigation. But how was anyone to know of Hunter's mother-in-law's connection to Lonergan? And what difference did it make anyway?

"Well, that was most productive I must say," chirped McClean. "What a lovely young lady."

"Did you know that Inspector Lonergan is a brother of Hunter's mother-in-law, McClean?"

McClean looked nonplussed.

"First I knew of it," continued Gwen. "I mean, how could we have known?" She knew she was speaking to thin air. McClean had a far-away look in his eyes.

At some level Gwen felt as if she was pre-empting her next conversation with Morecamb and rehearsing what she should say.

"Could you repeat that thing you said about the Lonergans, Gwen? I may have misheard."

The truth was that he was still buzzing after his delightful conversation with Isabelle…. "double 'l' followed by an 'e'" and he was having difficulty focussing.

"You heard. And I'm not repeating myself."

Suddenly she sprang forward and brought her fist down on the desk. "Lonergan is a brother of Mrs Bishop except _____."

"Who's Mrs Bishop?"

"She's not Mrs Bishop, she kept her maiden bloody name when she married." Another thump on the desk. "She still goes by her maiden name of Lonergan."

McClean had no idea where this was going but he felt it prudent to ask a few questions and try to jolly her along.

"So who is Mr. Bishop married to?"

McClean felt that was a reasonable question and certainly didn't warrant Cassidy's explosive response. Tentatively he bent down to retrieve all the documents and various correspondences which now littered the floor, not forgetting the telephone which was now in several pieces.

Gwen stormed off to get a coffee, to cool herself down she said.

Imagine! Whoever heard of a person drinking coffee to cool down, McClean pondered as he watched a red trickle of blood ooze from his hand. He hadn't noticed the smashed glass in amongst the general debris and he might now have to rush to A&E to get it stitched. He began to feel faint as the flow of blood began to gather pace and he hurriedly reached for his own phone and called a taxi.

While he waited for it to arrive, *'10 minutes, sir',* after he had explained that it was an emergency, he took the opportunity to call the hospital to alert them of his impending arrival.

Just as he was about to enter through the doors of A&E he suddenly remembered his conversation with Isabelle and her revelation that Hunter had been having an affair with a fellow police officer, who had got herself in 'the family way'.

Well, there was a motive right away.

"Poor Geoffrey felt he had been duped", Isabelle had said, "and the woman actually had expected him to leave his wife and marry her. Well, I ask you! Would you, Sergeant McCain?"

Good lord, that didn't bear thinking about. Poor Superintendent Hunter. And in her distraught state poor Isabelle had got his own name wrong which was perfectly understandable in the circumstances.

CHAPTER 26

Morecamb's and Nagle's trip to the mortuary proved fruitless as they had to contend with the anodyne assistant, Jeremy. They communicated through the frosted glass on the outside door and were informed that Jane was unavailable and "hadn't left a forwarding address." Morecamb heard Nagle struggling to stifle a laugh. Morecamb, meanwhile, was struggling to avoid putting his fist through the pane of glass. Nothing for it but to get back to the station.

As they approached the Incident Room they noticed the trail of blood leading from the corridor right up to one of the desks.

"What's gone on here?" Morecamb asked Cassidy who had her head down and was feverishly writing.

"I have no idea, sir. I just went into the canteen to get a coffee and when I came out I saw the blood and there's no sign of McClean. So I can only assume it's his blood. Oh, and I found a broken glass on the floor so perhaps he had some kind of accident."

"And you mean he didn't tell the whole world?" asked Morecamb. "That's not like him. Do you know if he got a chance to phone Hunter's in-laws?"

"Yes, sir, he was speaking to the sister."

"And?"

"Well, he said it went very well but he didn't elaborate."

"Again, that's not like him," said Morecamb.

"Maybe he tried to make a date with her, she spurned him and he ripped into his veins with a broken glass," opined Nagle.

"And," said Morecamb, "yet again he would have informed the whole world before the act. How did you get on, Gwen?"

"Yes, I spoke with both in-laws, that is to say the father and mother. Obviously neither held him in high regard. The father-in-law described him as a gold digger and a very inferior match for his daughter."

"Do you think he could be a suspect?"

"Not really. He obviously couldn't stand the man but it was his table manners and his lofty notions that seemed to irk him most. Hardly a motive for murder."

"And what about the wife?"

"Well, I've been thinking about that. She seemed far more reticent to condemn Hunter and she actually said very little about him."

"Do you think we should bring her in for questioning?"

"It might be no harm."

When to drop the bombshell, Gwen wondered as she felt a sheen of perspiration on her forehead.

Suddenly she spotted the approach of McClean and saw an opportunity.

"Right, get onto Mrs Bishop and ask her to come in," Morecamb said as he turned on his heel and headed for the door. He had it half open when Gwen called out, "Mrs Bishop retained her maiden name, sir."

"So?"

"She still goes by the name of Lonergan, sir."

He had a second leg out the door when he stopped and screamed, "What did you say?"

McClean, who was walking gingerly, with his bandaged hand up in the air decided to walk on by and pretend he was unaware of the tsunami which seemed about to erupt. But Morecamb yanked him by the collar and marched him into the room.

"Sit there, McClean and don't utter a bloody word. If you mention your hand I'll chop it off."

For once the sergeant obliged. Then Morecamb rounded on Gwen and in a tremulous voice she recounted her exchange with Mrs Hunter/Lonergan.

Morecamb was stunned.

"Get up, McClean, I need to sit down."

McClean gladly obliged and went to the furthest end of the room. Instinctively he felt that this might not be the time to mention the other woman in Hunter's life.

"So," continued Morecamb, "let me get this straight. Lonergan and Hunter's mother-in-law are brother and sister. Why are we only finding out about this now? Why didn't the widow mention it? We asked her if she had met the people who were with her husband and to the best of my recollection she said she only met them, infrequently, at social events. Am I right, Gwen?"

"That's correct, sir".

"Do you think she deliberately omitted that information, boss?" asked Nagle.

"I've no idea but I intend finding out. McClean, ring Mrs Hunter and tell her to get her arse in here first thing Monday morning."

McClean held his injured hand up in the air and pointed towards it with his good hand.

Morecamb glared at him. "Right, let's hear it and the short version, please."

"Well, sir, there was a bit of a kerfuffle of an exaggerated nature, I might add _____."

"Short version, please."

"Right. So, the broken glass on the floor…..I didn't notice it at first but as I picked it up _____."

"You've two minutes."

"So it necessitated a trip to A&E and, believe it or not, I was told to wait while they dealt with the more serious cases _____."

"I believe it."

"Anyway, it wasn't until I fainted that they….I want to say 'manhandled'…..me into a cubicle and a black doctor came in……..

Racist as well, thought Morecamb.

"………and told me I didn't need stitches. This precipitated a stand-off. Eventually, he agreed to put a bandage on it and then called Security. Needless to say I shall be talking to my solicitor."

"Good. In the meantime get onto Mrs Hunter _____."

"Sir," interrupted Gwen, "she's gone on holidays, remember?"

"My God," sighed Morecamb, "where will it end! Right, McClean, I believe you spoke to the sister of the deceased. The short version, please."

"Well, I may need to consult my notes."

There was an audible gasp in the room. Even McClean realised that an instant response was desirable.

"Or maybe not," continued McClean. "First off, let me say what a lovely person. Isabelle is her name, that's with a double 'L' and an 'E' at the end _____."

Morecamb brought his fist down on the desk and a glass teetered on the edge of the glass.

"Yes," hurried McClean, "and she was very forthcoming on all his virtues. Patient, kind, generous, held in very high regard by his peers"…………….he realised he was now babbling…….. "a loving husband, incapable of being deceitful and would never even consider having an extra-marital affair."

Christ, thought Morecamb, *he really must have lost a lot of blood.*

"Right, you can shut up now. So she was obviously no use at all. A bit like yourself in fact. Nagle, what do you make of this connection between the Lonergans?"

"Well, I think it's damned suspicious, to say the least. But they must have known that we would find out."

"Okay, let's recap. Hunter, Lonergan and Hunter's mother-in-law are all connected. I've asked Alderton and Murphy, God help us, to delve into Lonergan's background. Sullivan, will you go and bring those two gentlemen up here. Use force if needs be. Somebody ask the Superintendent if she can spare a few minutes. Gwen, did you get any information at all from Mrs Lonergan or Bishop…..bloody hell, this is confusing."

"Well, I gather Mrs Bishop comes from a very wealthy background. She spoke about surrendering her wealth to her husband when she married him and it was in that context that I found out that she had retained her maiden name. She said that she had surrendered enough and she had no intention of surrendering her identity."

She was interrupted by the sullen entrance of Alderton. Murphy looked more buoyant and gave Morecamb a big wink. They were immediately followed by Thornhill.

"So, what's going on here, then?" she asked as she approached.

Morecamb briefly explained the latest disclosure and then turned to Alderton.

"I asked yourself and Murphy to look into Lonergan's background……"

"Allow me," said Murphy and Alderton let him off. However, half-way through his spiel, when Murphy mentioned the C.I.A. he was ordered to leave the room. Delighted, Alderton took up the story.

"Well, first up I think I already mentioned during my interrogation that he's a man of impeccable taste. A connoisseur of fine wines _____."

"See what I have to put up with," roared Morecamb.

"Let him finish, Detective Inspector," snapped Thornhill. "Carry on, Sergeant."

"My pleasure," purred Alderton. "Anyway, he is the scion of a very notable family who made their fortune in shipping. His father, Sir Wallace Lonergan, now deceased, made his fortune during the Second World War and continued to accumulate vast wealth after the war."

"Shipping what?" asked Morecamb.

"I'm getting to that," snapped Alderton. "I believe he was an invaluable asset, during those turbulent years, to the Allies and facilitated the transportation of arms and artillery, often running the gauntlet of the Hun. Fortunately, he was never torpedoed or came to any harm. And of course he was knighted for his selfless endeavours."

"There was an inquiry," Murphy piped up.

All heads swivelled in his direction. He was over by the door, making himself as inconspicuous as possible but now felt duty-bound to join in the conversation. Furthermore he had done all the work into Lonergan's background, well, most of it anyway, and he wasn't going to let Alderton take all the glory. He hadn't considered any possible fall-out or explosions.

"What did you say, Murphy?" demanded Morecamb.

Murphy shuffled forward, instantly regretting his initial outburst.

"Well, it's just that after the war there was some sort of inquiry into Lonergan."

"Stuff and nonsense," interjected Alderton.

"Shut up, Alderton. Carry on, Murphy."

"Yes, well, as I tried to tell you earlier the C.I.A. got involved. They contacted their counterparts in Britain but as Lonergan was already knighted the powers in London shut down the inquiry."

Murphy felt quite weak after his delivery. It wasn't often he had such an attentive audience so he shoogled McClean aside and sat in his chair.

"That's very good work, Murphy," said Morecamb with a distinct note of incredulity in his voice. "And who was your source for all this?"

"Well, I'm not at liberty to say, Boss, you know _____."

"David Blake," interrupted Alderton, miffed that he was being sidelined and beginning to regret his earlier command to Murphy to contact his source. But there was the earlier indiscretion with Blake's wife, a long time ago, admittedly, but he felt that Blake was the type to hold a grudge.

"Who's he?" asked Morecamb.

"He's an old acquaintance of mine," said Alderton. "Retired now but he had a fairly senior position within M.I.5."

"Interesting," said Morecamb. "So, he's British. I know someone who might be able to make some discreet enquiries. So, is it just two children that Lonergan Senior had?"

"Yes," said Murphy, "a son and a daughter. The son is our friend, the Inspector and the daughter is Hunter's mother-in-law. And, get this", said Murphy, warming to his theme and all things conspiratorial, "isn't she married to a Mr. Bishop but _____."

"Retained her maiden name of Lonergan," Morecamb finished for him. "And what about Inspector Lonergan? Is he married?"

Murphy was now standing and, for the second time in his life, he had an audience. Once again Alderton thought it was time to intervene.

"He was married but it only lasted a few months. I believe they got a Church annulment."

"How do you get that?" Morecamb asked, suddenly remembering his own situation with his ex-wife, Fiona and his now precarious relationship with his pregnant girlfriend. Fiona had assured him that they were divorced but he'd never followed up on it.

"No idea," said Murphy, the germ of an idea beginning to form in his mind. Alderton was on a similar track.

"I believe if the marriage isn't consummated then you can get a Church annulment," volunteered Gwen.

"That's interesting," said Morecamb. "Nagle, will you try to track down the ex-wife and see what she has to say. See if you can get her to come into the station. Preferably Monday morning sometime."

"No problem, boss."

"Right, I think it's time we called it a day. Thank God it's the weekend. So, first thing on Monday we'll tackle the Lonergan woman. See what that throws up. See you all on Monday."

CHAPTER 27

Twenty minutes later Gwen arrived home. Well, maybe the word 'home' might be an exaggeration but at least it was a space where she could attempt to process the day's events.

She was tempted to have a stiff whiskey but decided she'd need a clear head to think through everything.

She was torn between keeping silent on the one hand and revealing all on the other.

Telling Morecamb about her relationship with Hunter was a huge risk. She would obviously be thrown off the case but it also occurred to her on the way home that it was possible she would be considered a suspect. She couldn't bear that. She had gone through enough as a result of her relationship with Hunter and she didn't feel she should suffer any further. Maybe she'd have that whiskey after all.

When McClean had stood up to speak earlier she was terrified that her secret would be revealed. As she finished her second whiskey she thought back over what he had said about Hunter's so-called 'fidelity'.

It was a strange thing to say, even for McClean, and she had felt a deep sense of dread. She would have to tackle him in the morning and find out exactly how the conversation with Hunter's sister had gone. She would have to be discreet, of course. God alone knew what McClean would do if he suspected her involvement with the dead man.

She pulled the bottle of whiskey towards her and decided to "have one for the ditch", as her father was fond of saying.

God, but it was dreary here. She surveyed her surroundings. A heavy pall descended on her. The wallpaper was peeling at every corner, there was damp on the back wall and, though she should have changed the miserable light bulb teetering in its moorings, she had decided against it. She knew that the feeble light camouflaged the worst excesses of years of neglect and decay. Hopefully her stay in this dump would be temporary.

She wouldn't bother to get the dripping tap fixed or replace the tattered curtains. It simply wasn't worth it. Morosely she wondered if anything was worth anything.

God, she sighed, things should be so different. How had she visualised it? Even in her current maudlin fog she could never visualise herself as Mrs Hunter. Had she ever really believed it? But her unborn child had been real enough and now she gave into the "what might have been."

Her daughter, it had been a girl, would now be sleeping contentedly in her little cot. Gwen would be carefully folding her little dresses and tiny socks and placing them neatly in a drawer. Mornings would have meaning, something to get up for. She visualised her little girl eagerly standing up in her cot, beaming, her chubby little arms raised to be lifted and cuddled. She would brush her wispy hair tenderly from her forehead, kiss her dimpled cheeks and tell her she was "the bestest girl in the whole world."

A lump lodged in Gwen's throat and she felt that no amount of time could possibly dislodge it. As she stumbled towards her bed, with the whiskey bottle tucked under her arm she could feel the tears coursing down her cheeks. There was no need to turn on the light in her bedroom. Daylight and night-time were all the same.

*****

Morecamb was dreading the reception which awaited him as he pulled up outside his house. All the lights were on which meant that Jane was home. He slowly got out of the car and locked the door.

As soon as he entered the hallway he could smell the aroma of cooking. So far, so normal, he hoped. Jane was clattering about the kitchen and gave a muted response to his greeting. When he said he was going to freshen up she ignored him and, as he climbed the stairs, he knew he should have asked her how she was feeling before attending to his own needs. But he didn't know how to broach the subject and was hoping that Jane would take the lead.

That obviously wasn't going to happen and he wondered if he would ever regain even a modicum of that now, long-dead excitement of fatherhood. Back then he'd had no reservations. Quite the opposite. He could have delivered several lectures on the joys of impending fatherhood. Written a bloody book on the topic, he mused, as he yanked at his tie and threw his jacket on the bed.

Fifteen minutes later, and with no small amount of trepidation, he re-entered the kitchen. Jane was still attacking the cutlery and crockery and he noticed that the table had just one setting on it.

"Have you eaten already?" he asked.

"No, I couldn't face it."

"But, it's fish. Isn't it?"

"Yes."

"But I thought you _____."

"Well, you thought wrong. Tea and toast is the highlight of my dietary consumption."

"Maybe you should see a doctor," Morecamb offered. No sooner had the words left his mouth than Jane flung the tea towel in the sink and dashed upstairs in floods of tears.

Suddenly Morecamb's appetite deserted him and somewhere in the deep recesses of his mind he remembered a chapter on pregnancy that he had read. God, it seemed a life-time ago. It pontificated about hormones and mood shifts and cravings. In all honesty he couldn't remember if it mentioned starvation.

Slowly he climbed the stairs, knocked gently on the bedroom door and entered without waiting for a response. Jane was faced towards the wall and was crying softly.

Morecamb sat on the edge of the bed and waited for the tears to subside.

"What do you want?" she gulped.

"We need to talk, Jane. We need to thrash things out."

"Is that how you see our baby?" she screamed. "As something that needs to be thrashed out?"

"Don't be ridiculous." He regretted the words as soon as they were aired.

The weeping started all over again and suddenly Morecamb began to lose patience. Jane wasn't some child who needed to be cossetted and cajoled. She was a bloody adult and carrying on like this was getting them nowhere.

"Listen to me, Jane. All this nonsense has to stop."

She whirled around towards him but before she could speak he ploughed on.

"This is a major event in both of our lives. No, let me finish. If either of us goes off on a rant we'll be no further on. This is not something we had planned for but now that it has happened we do need a plan. I think it's called, "closing the stable door when the horse has already bolted" and, no, you're not the stable and the baby isn't a horse. At least, not yet," he added jokingly but he quickly pressed on when he saw the scowl on Jane's face. "We're in this together and the sooner we start working as a couple the easier it will be."

Jane seemed to have calmed down and suddenly she breached out and took his hand.

"So tell me how you really feel about the whole thing?" she asked.

"How I feel?" he echoed. He looked at her tear ravaged face and was tempted to offer platitudes. But there was no point. It would be counter-productive to start this journey with a lie.

"I honestly don't know," he answered truthfully. "I'm forty two years of age and I never envisaged myself as a father at this stage."

"Well, you're not old, at least not entirely ancient."

Morecamb could detect the hint of a smile behind her words.

"Well, I'm not young either. But that's neither here nor there now. Look, what's the first thing we need to do? I mean, don't you have to make an appointment with a gynaecologist or something?"

"See! You're not as much of a green-horn as you think!" said Jane animatedly. "Actually I went to my G.P. this afternoon _____."

"Oh, I wondered where you were. I went by the mortuary this afternoon with Nagle but I met that knob, what's-his-name?"

"God, I hope you didn't torment him or threaten him. I might need to lean on him in the coming months."

"No, I was impeccably behaved. We didn't even go inside. So, what did the doctor say?"

"Well, she's going to book me in for a scan as soon as possible and then _____."

"What's a scan?"

"Have you never heard of one?" Jane asked incredulously. "It's like an x-ray of the womb and you can see the foetus and hopefully the heart beat."

"Wow!" Morecamb began to feel the first stirrings of excitement. Smiling he reached out and took Jane in his arms.

"We're going to be okay," he whispered into her hair. "Everything is going to be just fine."

CHAPTER 28

The ex- Mrs Lonergan was due to arrive at the station in half an hour, Detective Nagle informed Morecamb. "Interestingly, she has moved back to Cork, obviously to get as far away as possible from her ex but she also grew up here so I guess it was a natural move. Oh, and she's reverted to her maiden name. She's Margaret O' Driscoll now."

"My God," Morecamb sighed, "what is it with these women! Arriving in half an hour? It's only 8 o' clock. Why so early?"

"Well, she works in City Hall and what with the traffic and everything she doesn't want to be late."

"Okay. We'll put her in Interview Room 1 and make sure the heating is turned on in there. It's bloody freezing in here. I'll be along in a minute. I've a phone call to make and I want to grab a coffee."

He was hopeful that Lonergan's ex could shed some light on the man. He had a terrible feeling that the investigation had stalled and, before long, O' Toole would insist on removing him from the investigation or, worse still, close it down altogether and stamp 'Accidental drowning' on the file.

He headed to his office and dialled Drummond's personal number. It was answered on the fourth ring.

"Jim! Good to hear from you. Bit early though, isn't it? Please tell me there's been a development."

Morecamb went on to tell him about the Lonergan connection.

"Wow!" said Drummond, "I had no idea. But…..what's the significance? I don't see any advantage for the parties to conceal it or am I missing something?"

Morecamb had to agree with him but said he didn't believe in coincidences.

Drummond laughed. "I see you haven't forgotten your training all those years ago. I too can remember that mantra though I have to say that over the years I've tended to dismiss it. I've seen plenty of cases where coincidences have proved utterly innocuous. But, carry on. Anything else?"

"Well, the main reason I want to talk to you is to pick your brain about a chap called David Blake."

"Never heard of him. Should I have?"

Morecamb told him about Alderton's connection and his revelation regarding MI5.

Drummond roared out laughing and it took a few minutes for the laughter to subside. For some reason Morecamb began to feel a little miffed.

"Oh, come on, Jim. Alderton? Seriously?"

"Well......"

"Look, do you seriously think this Blake guy would entrust Alderton with that kind of information? Seriously?"

"Well, Blake is retired now so _____."

"But he'd still be sworn to whatever secrecy code those guys swear to uphold," reasoned Drummond.

"Yes, I hadn't thought of that." Morecamb could hear the doubt in his own words. "But isn't there a possibility that someone like Blake might feel short-changed by the organisation if it failed to act on the suspicious circumstances of the senior Lonergan's wealth?"

"I doubt it after all these years," said Drummond. "In fact I think it's very possible that there is no such guy as this Blake fellah."

"Why so?" asked Morecamb.

Drummond could detect a sharpness in Morecamb's tone.

"Well, no reason I suppose, nothing concrete at least. Look, I'll ask around, discreetly of course, and I'll get back to you. Don't worry, Jim, if there's a scintilla of truth in it I'll get back to you straight away."

There were no goodbyes or promises to visit as soon as possible. In fact there had been an awkwardness in their exchange and Morecamb felt annoyed about that. Once again the spectre of the dastardly Alderton was spreading its shadow and tainting everything in its orbit.

On his way to join Nagle in the interview room he ran into Thornhill. Their exchange was frosty and, in an effort to appease the woman he updated her on his call with Drummond.

Just the bare outline of course but he didn't mention Drummond's scepticism about Alderton. He also informed her about the upcoming interview with Lonergan's ex.

"Let me know how you get on," she said as she turned abruptly and continued on her way.

CHAPTER 29

The former Mrs Lonergan was already seated in the room, with a cup of coffee, when Morecamb joined her and Nagle.

She was a woman in her early forties, he reckoned, but her grey hair made her look older. She was dressed in a tweed jacket and navy slacks, the typical uniform of a Civil Servant. There were two very pronounced lines on either side of her mouth with a distinct downward trajectory, giving her a solemn and rather sad appearance.

Somehow he couldn't imagine her as Lonergan's partner. There was something almost deflated about her and her hands seemed to have a life of their own. They were constantly twitching and every so often she sought to control them by putting them on her lap. But, almost immediately, they were back up on the table again and she seemed to look at them with bewilderment.

A nervous witness then, Morecamb mused, which could go either of two ways. Nagle seemed to sense her nervousness as well and he introduced her in a gentle tone, before giving a warning frown to Morecamb.

"Thanks for coming in, Miss O Driscoll. May I call you Margaret?" asked Morecamb.

"Please do."

"I understand you were married to Inspector Lonergan?"

"Yes."

"Can you tell me for how long? I believe it was for quite a short period of time."

"That's correct." The hands were back on her lap again and there was a damp imprint on the table where they had fluttered momentarily.

"Was there a specific reason or just general incompatibility?"

"Yes. That. Incompatibility."

"There's really no need to feel nervous, Margaret," said Morecamb as he now detected a tremor in her voice. "You're not in any kind of trouble."

"Is my ex-husband?" Both men noticed that she didn't call him by his Christen name. Of course he probably wasn't a Christian at all, at least none that any church would lay claim to, Morecamb mused.

"Not as far as we are aware," Nagle answered though it didn't seem to make her any more at ease. "But I suppose we would class him as a person of interest in a case we're investigating."

"Have you heard or read about the sailing incident in Kinsale?" asked Morecamb.

"Yes, but my ex-husband didn't have anything to do with what happened."

Both men paused for a moment to let that bit of information sink in.

"I know we weren't married for very long _____."

"Five months," Morecamb interjected.

"Yes, but I feel that I know him well enough and he wouldn't dream of doing anything as awful as killing a man."

"So, he told you about the circumstances surrounding the death of Superintendent Hunter?"

There was a slight hesitation before she nodded and the hands went back to her lap again.

"Are you in regular contact, Margaret?" asked Nagle.

"No. Well, I mean every now and then." The nervousness was more pronounced now.

"But this was one such occasion?" pressed Nagle.

"Well......yes...but why not? I'm sure he was very upset.....in fact I know he was. And, after all, we were married _____."

"For just five months," Morecamb supplied. "What else did he say about the incident? Did he give you any specifics?"

"No."

"Somebody mentioned that you had got a Church annulment. How does that work?" asked Morecamb, "or how did it work in your case?"

"Our marriage wasn't consummated but I don't want to discuss anything about that." There was a steeliness in her voice now and also a touch of anger. "It's nobody's business."

"Of course not but I'm a curious sort," said Morecamb as he deliberately held her gaze. "Can I ask which of you initiated proceedings?"

"We both did. We both decided to get married and we both decided to separate." She still held Morecamb's gaze.

"That must have been difficult for you," said Nagle.

"How do you mean?" she asked, turning to look at Nagle.

"Well, I suppose it's a little unusual. You know, to walk away from a marriage and admit that it was a failure."

"Well, it wasn't my fault that it failed," she snapped. "How the hell was I to know......."

"Know what?" prodded Nagle, as she suddenly stopped in mid-sentence.

"Nothing." Then she barked out an angry laugh. "Yes, you could say I knew absolutely nothing."

"What about his family? Were you close to any of them?" asked Morecamb.

"No, I wasn't. My ex was fairly close to his sister. Actually she's the mother-in-law of that dead Superintendent or whatever. But I suppose you know that already. Yes, they were in contact quite a bit. Stands to reason considering they inherited the family business though I think she's the brains of the outfit. I never liked her but then she never liked me either. Thought I wasn't good enough."

"And what about her husband? Mr. Bishop. Is he involved in the business?" asked Nagle.

"Not at all!" scoffed Margaret. "He's just a pompous oaf. Old man Lonergan only agreed to his daughter's marriage to him on condition that Bishop never got his hands on the business."

"So, is she the main player in the business then?" asked Morecamb. "I mean what about your ex?"

"Oh, he's just an errand boy," she answered bitterly. "I'm not saying he's short of a few bob and I must say he's been very generous to me lately."

"More generous than usual?"

"Well......maybe."

"But not always?"

"Well, he wasn't exactly flush before we married but I didn't mind. I was in love, you see. But his old man kept a tight rein on the money and he couldn't stand my ex, his own son! More or less disowned him."

"Oh? Any idea why?"

"No, I've no idea. It was a few years before I married him although as soon as we married I think things thawed a little between them. At least he was at our wedding. But my husband didn't talk much about it. In fact he said nothing at all."

"And how did the old man react when the marriage ended?" asked Nagle.

"He didn't. He was dead by then. He died about three months after our wedding."

"So that cleared the way for your ex to join the company?"

"Well, yes, but I think his role is fairly minimal. Still, he's able to trade on the name so he's not complaining. That sister of his holds the purse strings now. Look, I have to go. I can't afford to be late."

Both men accompanied her to the door. Nagle offered to drive her but she informed him that she had her own car now, curtesy of her ex-husband.

As she turned on the ignition she resolved to ring her ex as soon as she got in to work about the interview she had just endured. After all he did buy the car for her. She knew it had been a sort of bribe so that she wouldn't disclose the real reason behind the failure of their pathetic marriage. In his last phone call he seemed terrified of being blackmailed and had muttered something about the boss's ability to bring pressure to bear on him.

Margaret hadn't a clue where all this was coming from but instinctively she felt it was somehow connected to events in Kinsale.

CHAPTER 30

The phone-call came at 12.40.

Thornhill had been half expecting it.

You didn't spend six years in the claws of the Mafia and hope that there wouldn't be some kind of backlash.

It was stupid of her to think that by coming to Ireland she could out-run her past. There was always someone willing to take you down, some-one who had the ability to cut through all the secrecy. And, invariably, it was someone who was probably a lot more corrupt than anyone else.

Oh, he knew all about her "little secrets", he informed her with a sneer in his voice......an inside informant giving advance warning to the enemy about raids and shake-downs. Of course he could understand her reasons. Owing that amount of money to "people like that" was every-one's worst nightmare.

So it was quite understandable that she had settled for "payment-in-kind". Hell, he quite understood that. He would have done the same himself.

Gambling, wasn't it? And he understood she had left the States under a cloud but wasn't it fortunate that her Uncle was Minister for Justice. He would be impacted as well of course if the whole sordid affair were to come out.

However, he could think of no reason whatsoever why it should be revealed. He just had a favour to ask of her.

"I want Alderton to be the fall-guy for Hunter's murder. I know I can rely on you."

CHAPTER 31

Gwen and Nagle had been dispatched to bring Mrs Hunter into the station. Thankfully she lived in Kildare so they didn't have to trek all the way to Dublin and face the traffic. Under ordinary circumstances Gwen would have been glad of the distraction but she was in dread at what the Bishop woman would say. Did she also know about Gwen's link with Hunter? She hoped that Nagle didn't notice that she was unusually quiet and tense.

Nagle had indeed picked up on the tension but, as a man who had been married for nigh on twenty years he knew better than to ask silly questions like, "Is everything okay?" when the person blatantly wasn't.

Mrs Bishop had refused to leave her house until her husband had phoned for her lawyer. Only when the lawyer agreed to meet her in the station in Cork did she condescend to travel.

When they got her back to the station, after a silent and tense journey, she was shown into a very cold interview room.

When Nagle asked Gwen to fetch a coffee for Mrs Bishop she didn't honestly feel that she could carry it without spilling the entire contents on herself. She had been tense on the outward journey but the return had almost snapped her in two. And now she was back worrying about the extent of information which the Bishop one had and how much she was willing to divulge.

God, would it never end? Would her past forever dog her footsteps? She felt angry and fearful in equal measure.

*****

While he waited Morecamb tapped out a beat on his desk and reflected on the conversation with Margaret O' Driscoll. Instinctively he felt that the Lonergans were key to the whole puzzle. But for the life of him he couldn't fit the pieces together. Maybe they could tease something out of the Bishop woman.

There was a light tap on the door and Nagle popped his head in.

"The Bishop woman is in the interview room and I think her lawyer has just arrived."

"Who is it this time?" he asked as he levered himself out of the chair. 'God I'm getting old' he thought and then he remembered that he was going to be a father soon and, in spite of his earlier twinge of excitement, he could feel the sweat coursing down his back at the thought. He was certainly in no mood for any theatrics from the Bishop woman.

"I don't know," said Nagle. "I haven't had the pleasure of meeting him yet."

"Benjamin Fleishman the Second," the voice boomed and a large meaty hand was extended to each of the men as they were about to sit down.

Morecamb introduced himself and Nagle and then he turned towards Mrs Bishop. "Thank you for coming in at such short notice," he said.

"I didn't have any choice, did I?" she answered curtly. "And of course the neighbours were having a field day. They didn't even try to hide their curiosity and one of them came out on the road to wave us off. Do you think I should sue, Ben?"

"Well, let's wait and see what these gentlemen have to say, shall we? Mmmm?"

Mrs Bishop sat up straighter in her chair, ready to do battle. The movement wasn't lost on Morecamb.

"Well, firstly, I'd like to ask you about your involvement in the family business. Shipping, isn't it?"

Of course she was happy to oblige. After all there was nothing sinister or illegal about the company that "Daddy" had founded, though how any of this related to the death of her son-in-law escaped her.

"Well", said Morecamb, "we don't know if there's a connection until we know more about the business."

"And do you really expect to instantly understand the complexities of the business considering your lack of knowledge and expertise in the area?" she snapped. "It's rather a leap from your dubious expertise in law and order to understanding the world of commercial enterprise."

"Well, we were hoping," said Morecamb, "that there might be an overlap, Ma'am, between your intricate enterprise and the upholding of law and order."

There was a sharp in- take of breath and she reminded Morecamb of a bull stamping its feet, nostrils flared before charging at some unsuspecting by-stander.

"Are you going to sit there twiddling your thumbs for the afternoon, Ben?" she asked turning on her lawyer. "Lord knows we pay you enough to contribute to this ridiculous charade."

"I suggest that you listen to what these gentlemen have to say and answer their questions as comprehensively as possible", Fleishman replied calmly.

He wasn't going to be brow-beaten by this witch! He had long suspected that she was involved in some fairly shady deals and he had every intention of severing connections with the lot of them. The only reason he was still representing them was the promise he had made to his father who had founded the practice. The poor man had been constantly re-minded of the debt of gratitude owed to old man Lonergan for saving so many Jews from 'the incinerators'.

He was still irked by her husband's attitude on the phone earlier, the final straw which cemented his intention to quit. It had been nothing short of outrageous. He suspected there may have been drink involved, at 11 o' clock in the morning, but that was no excuse.

The man was habitually arrogant and demanding and was an abso-lute embarrassment when their paths crossed on social occasions. Yes, he would miss the fees but some things weren't worth the price. "If you cooperate as fully as possible, Mrs Bishop," Fleishman continued, "we won't find ourselves back here at a moment's notice when I, for one, have other business to attend to."

She recoiled a little at the sharpness in his voice but Morecamb and Nagle, for the first time in their life, experienced a grudging respect towards the legal cabal.

There were tears of rage in her eyes when she turned back towards Morecamb.

"Right, get on with it."

"What sort of cargo do you transport?"

"A mixture," she answered vaguely.

"Be specific."

"Coffee, sugar, crude oil, petroleum, timber, cotton, wheat", she rattled off.

"Ports of origin, please?"

"Argentina, Brazil, Columbia, North America, Eastern Europe, mainland Europe". She was like a bold child reciting her ten times tables but Morecamb wasn't fazed.

"And where in Ireland do you usually dock?"

"Where do you think? Dublin Port, of course."

"Not Cork or Belfast?"

"Rarely Cork, definitely not Belfast. We'd prefer not to be blown to bits, thank you very much! And I don't think my partners would appreciate............"

"Partners?" asked Morecamb as she came to an abrupt stop.

"Well," she stammered, "you know what I mean. Stakeholders and that."

"Stakeholders?"

"My God, you're like a bloody parrot. Yes, stakeholders. Occasionally we've had people who like to invest in the company."

"Names?"

"Really? You must be joking," she laughed. "Those people are very private individuals and I have no intention _____."

"Okay, okay, we get the message. So, let's get back to the merchandise you carry. How is it transported to other parts of Ireland when the ship docks at Dublin Port?"

"By rail and road, of course. How else do you expect?"

"And never by sea? Say in a smaller boat? Wouldn't it be just as easy to transfer the cargo onto smaller vessels and then just continue on to Cork and Belfast? Surely that would be much more economical and a lot less hassle?"

Mrs Bishop pursed her lips and stared straight ahead.

There followed a strained silence in the room and it was as if everybody was holding their breath. Morecamb pressed on.

"How involved was your son-in-law in all this?"

"Very little. We like to keep things within the family."

"What about your husband? What's his role?"

"Minimal. Occasionally he helps out in the office if the staff is under pressure. My husband prefers to enjoy the perks. 'Work' is a rather foreign concept to him.

"So, if I understand things correctly, this is a pretty big operation yet you're telling me that only yourself and your brother are the main players here. And it would seem to me, in view of your brother's 'day job'....upholding law and order...... his role is fairly peripheral. Do you seriously expect me to believe that?"

"You can believe what you like."

"Tell us about your father. No danger of breaking confidences here, I presume? I mean he's dead, isn't he."

"No need to be facetious. You're speaking about a man who was knighted for his services to the Allies during the war. You probably owe your existence to him."

"I must remember to thank him. It's been a blast so far. As I understand he was never arrested, had his ship torpedoed or impounded by the enemy. Not even a scratch, for his troubles. He seems to have been extraordinarily fortunate _____."

"Or very skilled, Inspector. We were very proud of him and still are. He breeched enemy lines several times, ran the gauntlet of the enemy several times, put himself in grave danger in order to ensure a ready supply of armaments…." She had built up a head of steam at this stage…… " sacrificed his life _____."

"Well, I'm sure it wasn't a one-man operation. He obviously had plenty of help too, plenty of experts who helped in no small way to ensure the safety of the cargo, maybe a certain immunity, perhaps?" asked Morecamb and there was no hiding the subliminal message in his statement.

It obviously hadn't escaped Mrs Bishop either.

Her reaction was instant and almost violent. She pushed back her chair and it banged off the far wall. She grabbed hold of Fleishman's briefcase and it swiftly followed the direction of the chair. Police files and folders were swept to the floor and then, as if nothing had happened, she calmly picked up her handbag and walked out of the room.

Fleishman retrieved his briefcase and as he walked past the two officers he announced, "She's hoping to be given a title as well, sort of hereditary. 'Lady' something or other, I presume. Though I doubt it would be for services to the State," he finished enigmatically.

"I think we deserve a spot of lunch, Nagle, and maybe a pint or two," said Morecamb as the door closed.

CHAPTER 32

While Morecamb and Nagle had been locked in battle with Mrs Bishop, Gwen had spent the morning trying to make contact with Hunter's brother. She was on the point of giving up when he answered.

Her head was pounding but McClean had refused to be the one to ring Hunter's brother. According to himself he was a lady's man and found them always willing to talk freely to him.

Gwen may have imagined it but she thought he had eye-balled her as he made that last comment. God, was she getting paranoid? Either way she would have to quiz McClean about his conversation with Hunter's sister. She couldn't cope with this uncertainty. She was on the point of giving up in her attempt to speak to the brother when, at last, he chose to answer the phone.

"Tom Hunter, speaking."

He sounded younger than his brother but had the same clipped tones. As the conversation had progressed, Gwen realised that the tones were fuelled by anger rather than any attempt to appear posh.

She had hardly finished the explanation for the call when Hunter had launched into a tirade. Infidelity had featured prominently. Anything that wasn't nailed down, apparently. And the richer his brother had become the more arrogant he became. When he'd been mainly dependent on his wife's largesse to fund his extravagant lifestyle he had toed the line. But, in the last year or so, that had all changed and his wife was as much a victim as anybody else. He didn't even try to hide his philandering.

God, the brother had gone on and on and by the time Gwen came off the phone she, too, was seething with rage. Before she tackled McClean she decided to have some lunch.

When she went into the canteen she was relieved to see it was empty. As she ate she could feel her anger begin to subside and decided to take the full hour for her lunch break.

As she was tidying up her tray McClean bounced into the canteen. Gwen seized her opportunity.

"McClean, I want a word. I've just come off the phone with Hunter's brother, Tom, and he tells a very different story from the one you presented yesterday to the team. Care to share?"

McClean hesitated for a moment and checked over each shoulder to make sure they were alone.

"Yes, well, I may have underplayed things a little."

"Go on."

"Isabelle did say that he was having an affair." Here Mclean stopped and looked down at his feet. When he looked back up again he noticed that Gwen had paled a little.

"Did she say with whom?" she asked in a low voice.

"Not exactly," he said, "but she did say it was with one of his own, a fellow police officer."

There was a silence.

Gwen could hear the distant traffic. As if in a trance, she realised there must be an incline outside the station as she could identify the bigger vehicles going down in gear before they rumbled up the hill.

"She didn't give any name," McClean continued, "but I got the impression that she's single and there might have been a baby or at least a pregnancy."

Silence settled again and now the sound of traffic receded further and was replaced by a whooshing sound in Gwen's ears.

"Are you okay?" asked McClean and she thought she detected a genuine concern in his voice.

"Ah, here you are," said Nagle as the door opened behind them. "The boss wants a quick meeting."

CHAPTER 33

Somehow Gwen found herself walking ahead of McClean and Nagle but, later, for the life of her she couldn't remember very much about that meeting.

Morecamb began by telling the team about the meeting with Mrs Bishop.

"Is she calling herself Mrs Bishop now, sir?" asked McClean.

"What in the name of God has that got to do with anything?" Morecamb shouted, eye-balling him.

But McClean stood his ground. After all he was in possession of some very important information.

"I just need it for my notes, sir. You may remember, from an earlier exchange, in this very room and not too long ago _____."

"Shut up, McClean."

"Do you think there is something suspicious about the shipping company, sir?" asked Sullivan.

"See, McClean, a sensible question. Well, we really need to find out more about old man Lonergan and then we need to take a look at their current business. Now, which one of you spoke to Hunter's brother?" Morecamb asked, looking around.

Gwen had completely zoned out, caught up in her own miserable world.

When there was silence she looked up and caught the end of Morecamb's question, something about phoning Hunter's brother. For some reason McClean fielded the question.

"That would be me, sir. I phoned Superintendent Hunter's brother. His name is Tom, quite an ordinary name, I feel. Anyway, there were no new revelations other than his obvious dislike for the dead man and some spurious allegations about his dead brother's illicit affair with his sister-in-law. That would be Tom's wife, sir."

"Well, we have another Lonergan coming in tomorrow. Inspector Lonergan this time. Hopefully we'll be a bit closer to unravelling this puzzle though I can think of no good reason for such optimism, more a case of desperation. Gwen, will you and McClean add all the characters and the various roles so far to the white board. Nagle, can you think of anybody that you could query about this man, Blake? Do it discreetly and steer clear of Headquarters for the moment. I'm going to my office to finish off paperwork. We'll knock off at five."

CHAPTER 34

Jennifer Bishop was incensed by the time her call was answered. She had been waiting twenty minutes and had spent that time pacing up and down the Drawing Room.

"You took your time," she snapped as she grabbed the phone on the second ring.

"Well, I'm a busy man, aren't I, between the lot of you. I'm now forced into a situation of damage limitation."

"Well, you're the one who insisted on Cuthbert being on board and I've just come back from the station, after spending an hour being interrogated."

"And your son-in-law was the one who insisted on Alderton being on board and that's where the problem is," he retorted. "What was it? Oh yes, 'trying to mend broken fences'. Well, that worked out well, didn't it," he added sarcastically. "Now he's the only one who can point the finger at Cuthbert."

"None of that is my fault," she bristled.

"You could have kept a tighter rein on your bloody son-in-law _____."

"How was I to know that he was suddenly going to develop a conscience and refuse to have anything more to do with our venture? I blame that affair he had with _____."

"Look," he interrupted, "Geoffrey had any amount of god-damned affairs _____."

"But this one got pregnant. That was the problem," she shouted down the phone. "Hunter wanted children but my daughter didn't want

any. And, obviously, when he found out she was pregnant he got all sop-
py _____."

"Well, he got a good promotion to keep his mouth shut and he was
bloody lucky because his track record wasn't exactly legendary."

"Look, all I know is that it was around that time that he started
talking about wanting out of the whole thing," she snapped back at him.

Jennifer Bishop could feel the hysteria rising as she visualised the
whole edifice come crashing down around her. Her caller, sensing this,
assured her that he had already set the wheels in motion and there was
nothing to worry about. He told her about his call with Thornhill. Alderton was going to take 'the fall'.

"And what about this woman that Geoffrey was having the affair
with? How sure can you be that he didn't confide something incriminating to her?" she asked, feeling no less hysterical.

"I'll take care of her," he answered abruptly and put the phone down.

CHAPTER 35

As soon as Morecamb arrived the following morning he was waylaid by a highly excited Alderton who was waiting for him outside his office door.

"Get in here, Morecamb."

"No, I won't. What do you want?"

"What's going on?" Alderton spluttered.

"Well, there are any number of things going on. Could you be more specific?"

"Lonergan!"

"What about him?"

"Exactly."

"As usual you're not making much sense, Alderton."

"Okay, I'll speak slowly. I have reason to believe that my good friend, Inspector Lonergan, is being dragged in to be shouted at by the likes of you."

Before he had a chance to answer Thornhill swooped down on them. She beckoned Morecamb to one side.

"I've just been informed that Superintendent Lonergan won't be here until the afternoon."

Morecamb swore under his breath. "Did he give a reason?" he asked.

"He doesn't have to furnish us with a reason. And I want you to remember that you will be interviewing a man who is equal in rank to you _____."

"I'll try to remember, Ma'am."

"I would say superior," interjected Alderton, "considering he's based in H.Q." said Alderton, spitefully.

"Sergeant Alderton, I'd be grateful if you'd return to the Cold Cases' unit," said Thornhill. "This is between Inspector Morecamb and me."

Morecamb almost felt sorry for his old adversary as he saw his face crumble and he sheepishly headed off down the corridor.

"Remember what I said, Morecamb. Show a bit of respect."

Morecamb was outraged as he watched her stalk off to her office. He found Nagle in the Incident Room and beckoned him outside.

"I've been instructed by the boss that I have to show respect for Lonergan which, obviously, won't be happening. Incidentally he's not arriving until this afternoon, for no good reason. But I suggest we go in hard on him and ignore Madam Thornhill. Who cares if Lonergan goes sobbing to her to complain."

"I gather we don't? Okay, you won't get any complaint from me."

"Right, I've got a phone call to make. Will you go and check on the others and I'll be in shortly."

Jane had been asleep when Morecamb had left in the morning and he wanted to check up on her. He caught her just before she left the house.

"Hey," he said as she answered.

"Hey, yourself. You're ringing early. Is everything ok?"

"Oh, yes, just checking to see if you're alright. You were a bit restless in your sleep last night."

"Yes, it took me ages to get off and when I did I kept wakening, trying to find a comfortable spot. I'm going to ring the doctor today and ask if there's any chance of an early scan."

"You're not worried, are you? I mean _____."

"No, God no. It's just to set my mind at rest. And yours too, obviously," she laughed. They chatted for a few more minutes and then Jane had to get off to work.

CHAPTER 36

Lonergan was a balding, 50 something year old and regarded both men with a supercilious grin before focussing his attention on the wall opposite to him. His suit screamed 'bespoke' and his shirt and tie hadn't fallen off any rack from some ordinary run-of-the-mill draper's.

The lawyer was similarly attired. He had a hawk-like appearance, the kind of species that would be immediately shot if he sprouted wings and took to the air.

"My name is Mr. Broderick," said the lawyer as he extended his hand, "and I sincerely hope that this interview isn't going to be adversarial. I'm aware of your reputation, Morecamb."

"This is Detective Nagle," said Morecamb, ignoring the lawyer's silly attempt at intimidation. "We're going to record this interview. Detective, will you do the honours?"

As soon as the little wheels started to whirr in the machine, Morecamb turned to Lonergan.

"So, Inspector Lonergan, we have your statement here _____."

"Is there a problem with it?" Broderick asked.

"Well, that's what we're here to find out."

Lonergan threw his eyes to the heavens.

"I'm intrigued by the events which unfolded as ye docked in Kinsale. You and Superintendent Wallace seem to have taken charge of the entire proceedings, even though one of your number had been murdered."

"Might I remind you that my client disputes that claim."

"It's a little difficult to deny the findings of the Post Mortem, I would have thought," smiled Morecamb. "At the very least, Inspector Lonergan, your actions were unorthodox."

"Needs must, old chap," drawled the lawyer. "As you're probably aware the particular personnel in Kinsale are, shall we say, a little challenged in their organisational skills as you know very well."

"Nevertheless, I'm going to read aloud Mr. Lonergan's statement for the tape."

"*Inspector* Lonergan," Broderick reminded them.

And so it continued, with the lawyer interrupting at every juncture until finally, in frustration, Morecamb threw the statement aside and addressed Lonergan directly.

"Tell me about your role in the family shipping business."

That got his attention and even Broderick's who seemed, momentarily, stuck for words. Lonergan drew himself up straight in his chair.

"I'd be delighted," he crowed. "The Company was started by my late father way back in _____."

"We know all that," interrupted Morecamb, "tell me about the merchandise you transport."

"Oh, you know, coffee, wheat, oil _____."

"Can you tell me about your role in the Company?" Now it was Morecamb's turn to interrupt. Meanwhile Broderick remained silent, with a perplexed frown marring his features, no doubt wondering, nervously, where all this was going.

"Oh, my role is obviously very important _____."

"Your sister doesn't think so. She certainly gave us the impression that you were very much on the margins, so to speak."

"My sister?" queried Lonergan.

"Yes, we also had your sister in here helping us with our enquiries."

"Well, let me tell you that my role is just as important as _____."

"Tell me about your relationship with your late father."

"My late father?" stammered Lonergan.

"I'd prefer if you didn't parrot my every question, to quote your sister."

"Well… em…. it was a normal relationship. I held him in very high esteem and I believe the feeling was reciprocated."

"Your ex-wife, who was also in here, tells a very different story."

"Well, in all fairness, Inspector, her opinion is hardly unbiased." Broderick had found his voice.

"Yes," continued Morecamb, "she told us you were estranged from your father for many years."

"Rubbish!" Lonergan was starting to get red around the gills.

"And," Morecamb continued, "it wasn't until your marriage that you became reconciled. Why was that?"

"My father didn't approve of my choice of wife and who could blame him," Lonergan said spitefully.

"Yet he attended your wedding. Let's get back to your role in the Company. Your sister told us that your role is very peripheral."

"How bloody dare she!" roared Lonergan.

"Toby, Toby", intoned Broderick, "calm down. There's no need _____."

"Let me tell you," interrupted Lonergan, "that Company would have hit the rocks a long time ago if it wasn't for me."

"And your ex-wife described your role as that of an errand boy. Or was it his sister who said that, Detective Nagle?"

Lonergan threw back his head and barked out an angry laugh. He reminded Morecamb of a wolf howling at the moon.

"Hit the bloody rocks," Lonergan shouted at Morecamb. "Diversify, she said. I was the one who suggested that years ago."

He sent his chair flying backwards as he leaned in towards Morecamb, spittle flying in all directions. We really should have the furniture nailed down, Morecamb thought.

"Toby, please," pleaded Broderick.

"Shut up," shouted Lonergan to his brief and he brushed his hand aside. "I bloody knew it was only a matter of time before the competition started making inroads on our enterprise. 'Ooooh, Toby', she said, 'you're in an ideal position to facilitate our new cargo,'" said Lonergan mimicking his sister. "She promised to make me a co-director. Well, I'm still waiting."

"When you say, 'new cargo' could you be _____."

"And let me tell you, she only thinks she's the boss. She doesn't get it all her own way, you know. Oh no, she does what she's told as well. 'Oooh, Toby, it's not possible to make you director at this juncture,'" he mimicked his sister again, " 'Mr Big has the final say, Toby dear'."

There were tears streaming down his face now and he gulped several times in an attempt to catch his breath.

"Mr. Bloody Big. He's no better than me. In fact I was in the force long before him. Fuck the lot of ye."

Incandescent with rage he stumbled to the door and almost took it off its hinges as he barged out. Morecamb heard Nagle announce to the tape that the interview had now concluded.

Broderick immediately got to his feet and marched out of the room in his client's wake, though with a lot more decorum.

Nagle turned to Morecamb as the door closed behind McIntosh. "Wow! Interesting, wouldn't you say?"

"Very," said Morecamb as he stared off into space. "I'm so bloody exhausted. What in God's name have we unearthed, Nagle?"

"God only knows."

"My head is spinning. I'll dismiss the team, give them an early evening and you and I will head to the pub. And we won't mention the bloody case again until we get back here in the morning."

*****

Thornhill was the last person to leave the station. She had thought long and hard about that earlier phone call. And, yes, she had agonised about the decision. But, strangely, once she had made up her mind a weight had lifted from her shoulders. Indecision was the killer, she told herself as she ripped the sketches which Melissa had drawn. She tore them into little pieces and dropped them in the bin. The cleaners would be in later and all trace would be removed.

CHAPTER 37

Morecamb and Nagle arrived into the Station car park at the same time the following morning.

"I've been thinking about the case," said Morecamb as they walked towards the entrance, "all bloody night, in fact. We need to talk to Alderton, informally, so we won't mention anything to the others just yet. Will you go and get him? His car is here so he's around somewhere and bring him to my office."

"What's going on now?" were Alderton's first words as he was ushered towards a chair in front of Morecamb's desk.

"We just want a few words."

"Well, do I need a whatsit, you know, a solicitor or something? If I remember correctly, the last time you spoke to me you said _____."

"No, no, nothing like that. This is just informal."

Alderton visibly relaxed and sat back in his chair, arms folded and one leg crossed over the other. He looked as if he hadn't a care in the world.

"You look stressed, Morecamb," he said with a smirk. "Not easy trying to function without my guidance, I dare say. You were never the most innovative of men. I was saying to Caroline, the other night _____."

"Alderton, you'll have to stop talking rubbish," interrupted Morecamb. "This is serious. At any stage, during your voyage off Kinsale, did anybody mention anything about a business venture?"

"What do you mean?"

"Was Lonergan, for example, boasting about his Company or his wealth or did he make any mention of his sister?"

"See, Morecamb, you have to understand that men of class don't go around boasting, as you call it, about.......what sister?"

"Mrs Bishop, Lonergan's sister."

"Never heard of her."

Morecamb wrapped his hands around his head and laid it on the desk. Then he emitted a loud groan and a string of curses.

"See," said Alderton turning to Nagle, "it's not easy. I knew he'd be completely out of his depth _____."

"Sergeant", said Nagle, taking over, "how sure are you that this Cuthbert man was on board? It's really important as the others have denied it."

"Look," said Alderton leaning forward, "Cuthbert was on board. I was talking to the bloody man for God's sake. He was English _____."

"That ties in with what Melissa said," said Morecamb.

"Who?" asked Alderton.

"Oh sweet Lord," breathed Morecamb.

"Go on about Cuthbert," said Nagle.

"As I said, he was definitely English. He spoke with a Cockney accent which kind of surprised me, if I'm honest _____."

"And which of the men seemed most familiar with him?"

"Well, certainly not Inspector Hunter, that's for sure. I got the impression that he didn't know him and he certainly wasn't aware that he would be on the trip. That doesn't surprise me, because, as I say the man seemed a bit rough around the edges and had a distinctly Cockney accent".

"And you're absolutely sure that this Cuthbert fellah bore no resemblance to any of the sketches that Melissa drew?"

"Who?"

"Slap him, will you, Nagle."

"Do you know," said Alderton conversationally, "I'm starting to remember more about the trip as time goes on? Isn't memory a strange thing? For example, I now remember that there was a loo on the upper deck so there was really no necessity for me to go traipsing all the way down below deck in my hour of need."

"Jim", said Nagle, "you'll to get back on to Drummond. Maybe he'd have the resources to track down _____."

"Who's Jim?" asked Alderton.

Suddenly they were rudely interrupted by the office door being slammed back against the wall and Thornhill came in looking like a mad bull.

"What the blazes is going on here, Morecamb?"

"Well," said Morecamb, calmly, "we're interviewing Sergeant Alderton _____."

"No, you're not. Can I have a word, please? Outside? Now!"

"See, you've upset Caroline now," said Alderton to Morecamb's retreating figure. "I've tried and tried......"

Morecamb shut the door on Alderton's monologue and turned to face his Superior. Her eyes were blazing.

"I want that man interrogated properly," she snarled, "with a solicitor present. I want the whole thing recorded, as per protocol, and if it's not done properly you and your side-kick in there will find yourselves back on the beat. Do I make myself clear?"

"Perfectly, Ma'am."

"I'll organise a duty solicitor," she raged on, "and I want it done this afternoon."

Morecamb felt as if a hurricane had blown through the corridor, leaving a very nasty chill in its wake. The corridor looked bereft as she made her exit. Morecamb looked around and suddenly felt frightened, as if everything was out of his control and he didn't understand his own role any longer. And, in the stillness, he knew that he and his team were mere pawns in a much bigger game.

He had an overwhelming desire to see Jane and talk about the new life they had created together, something pure and utterly untainted. Wasn't it strange, he thought, that the only solid thing he could hold onto right now was a mere speck that hadn't even come into existence yet?

Wearily he went back in to join the two men and relayed Thornhill's message about the re-scheduled interrogation. Alderton immediately bounced out of the chair and announced that he was going to apologise to Caroline and explain to her that none of this was his idea and he had been "forcibly coerced into attending this unorthodox meeting."

Morecamb didn't try to detain him, knowing that the big eejit would get a blast from both barrels when he went grovelling to Thornhill.

CHAPTER 38

Like Morecamb, McClean had also spent a restless night. He kept seeing Gwen's pale face as he had told her about Inspector Hunter.

He knew that most of his colleagues didn't hold him in high esteem. But that didn't dampen his enthusiasm for the job in any way. He had dreamed of being a Garda for a very long time, from his Primary School days, in fact.

He could still hear the taunts in the playground, the bullying as the other kids teased him about his absent father.

McClean didn't know who his father was or where he was. His mother never spoke of him. She would set her face in a thunderous scowl and send him to his room whenever he mentioned him. So, by the age of eight he had learned that his father was a forbidden topic and obviously a source of great pain to his mother.

In his final year in Primary he had learned the meaning of the word 'bastard' and he begged his mother to send him to a Secondary school on the other side of Cork city. It was fee paying but something in the set of his features had persuaded his mother to agree. He knew that she had taken on a second job as a cleaner in St. Finbarr's Hospital in order to afford it.

He should have been grateful but he felt it was the least he deserved. After all, it wasn't his fault that he had been 'born out of wedlock'. Yes, that was a new phrase he had learned in Secondary school, courtesy of Fr. Murphy on one of his regular rants at General Assembly.

But it was also here that McClean was able to carve out a new identity for himself. Now he watched other boys being bullied and teased, though he never joined in. Neither did he intervene, unwilling to draw attention to himself and become a target. Instead he resolved that one day he would be in a position of power. His mind was made up when, at a Recruitment Seminar in the school, he approached the Garda stall and took all the literature they had to offer.

He had never looked back and he had taken his new persona into his chosen career. A distant relation of his mother's, 'filthy rich' according to her, was now anointed as McClean's uncle and he had adopted all the trappings and wealth of his new, 'close' relation. McClean spoke at length, to anyone who would listen, about the beautiful summer home overlooking the bay in Garretstown.

That bit was true but the add-on about spending all his summer days there as a boy was the stuff of fiction. He had been there twice, for short periods but long enough for him to memorise every detail of the house and its surroundings.

Now, as he entered the Station he looked around for Gwen. As dawn had broken he had resolved that he would speak to her, put her mind at rest. He spotted her going into the canteen so he followed her and when he collected his coffee from the counter he went over and joined her in a quiet corner.

"What do you want, McClean?" she asked, without looking up. "I was hoping to have a quiet coffee before the mayhem starts."

Undaunted, McClean sat down and began his full story, from child-hood to the present day, warts and all. As he recounted it he was aware of a weight lifting from his shoulders. Gwen watched him, open-mouthed and could feel tears prickling behind her eyelids.

"I know most people here regard me as a fool," he said as he was coming to the end, "and I'm okay with that. But I don't want you to be the butt of some malicious jokes or rumours. I've guessed you are the woman that Hunter was seeing and perhaps even became pregnant....." He raised his hand as she started to respond. "I don't want to know as it's none of my business and I don't want to know about the baby or _____."

"I lost it," gulped Gwen in a whisper.

"I'm sorry. I just want you to know that your secret is safe with me and if you ever need to talk about it then I'll willingly listen. Sometimes that's all we need, someone to listen."

Gwen's tears overflowed and she buried her face in her hands and sobbed. She was vaguely aware of McClean leaving as he pressed a hand on her shoulder and quietly left the canteen.

*****

An hour later Morecamb called the team together and told them about the upcoming interview with Alderton. He was reluctant to call it an interrogation, partly out of an unfathomable respect for the man but also because he simply did not believe that Alderton was their culprit.

"Gwen, where are those sketches that the lass from Kinsale drew?"

"I gave them to Superintendent Thornhill, sir," she replied. "Shall I go and ask her for them?"

Morecamb, and indeed the rest of the team, had noticed the blotch-iness in Gwen's face. She had spent almost an hour in the ladies' cloak-room trying to restore her ravaged face and remove the twin-track of mascara which had stubbornly refused to budge.

Morecamb sincerely hoped that McClean hadn't been upsetting her again.

"Yes, Gwen, do that, please, and bring them along to the interview room. Number three, isn't it, Nagle?"

"That's right, boss."

Morecamb wasn't looking forward to this. A month ago he might have relished it but instinctively he felt that Alderton was as much a pawn as everyone else on the team, except, right now, Alderton seemed to have been elevated to the status of Rook, hemmed in on all sides by the other pieces and with severely restricted room to manoeuvre. And Morecamb felt that it wouldn't be any of the more powerful pieces that would topple him. No, that would be left to the pawns and the King and Queen would sit and wait patiently until they heard the word, 'Checkmate'.

CHAPTER 39

"Did you speak to Superintendent Thornhill, Sergeant?" asked Morecamb, as he and Nagle entered the Interview room. He was attempting to put Alderton at ease but he needn't have bothered. Alderton was calmness personified, helped no doubt, in no small measure, by the presence of his Brief, one of Cork's most eminent lawyers. Ben Frahill was sitting by his side. Morecamb had met the man once before and, whilst he didn't dislike him, he knew that he was an able adversary.

"No, she was busy," said Alderton a little sheepishly, "but she assured me that I would have her full attention later on. However, she did have time to secure a solicitor for me, a mere child fresh out of Law school, so I sent him away and asked Ben to represent me instead."

"I'm Detective Inspector Morecamb and this is Detective Nagle," said Morecamb extending his hand towards the lawyer.

"Benjamen Frahill," he responded, shaking hands with a firm grip. "I understand you're recording this, Inspector?"

"Yes, you've started the tape, Detective?" asked Morecamb.

"Yes, sir, up and running."

Morecamb suddenly felt very tired. God, they had been over this ground so many times. But, to Alderton's credit, he had never wavered from his original statement.

"Sergeant Alderton," began Morecamb, "I've asked one of my team to get the sketches of this Cuthbert man's likeness and I want you to take a good look at them again. I believe you said that one of the likenesses was a possibility."

"On the contrary, Morecamb, I believe I said that it looked like a monkey."

"Nevertheless, I want you _____."

He was interrupted by a knock on the door and Gwen's head appeared. "Can I have a word, please sir?"

Morecamb went to the door and poked his head out.

"I spoke with the Superintendent and she no longer has the sketches. She said she binned them after Sergeant Alderton couldn't make a positive identification."

"You've got to be joking!" spluttered Morecamb.

"She said she didn't like clutter, sir".

Morecamb re-joined the others, deep in thought. Why the hell would Thornhill do that? Okay, strictly speaking, one couldn't say that she had destroyed evidence….."

"Where are the sketches, Morecamb?" asked Alderton.

"Ahem, they're unavailable at the moment. We'll just carry on for the moment."

He could feel Nagle looking at him and he gave him, what he hoped, was an imperceptible shake of his head.

"Sergeant Alderton, you claim that you have very poor recollection of events in Kinsale. Could you estimate how much you had to drink or for how long were you drinking before you passed out?"

"I most certainly did not pass out," huffed Alderton.

"Can you answer the question, please?"

"Do I answer that, Ben, or will I just say, 'no comment'?"

"I suggest you answer it, Sergeant. After all you have nothing to hide."

"Well," said Alderton, "let's just say the alcohol was flowing freely. I couldn't honestly say how many drinks I had but enough, shall we say?"

"Shall we say, more than enough?" asked Morecamb.

"In retrospect, yes, perhaps," Alderton conceded.

"I want you to think very hard about the answer to my next question. Did you, at any stage, sense any tension among _____."

"No."

Thankfully the lawyer averted an explosion by leaning across and whispering in Alderton's ear.

"Look, everybody was a little squiffy, I dare say, but nobody was falling down drunk," said Alderton.

"And, just to reiterate, you're absolutely certain about this Cuthbert man?"

"Yes", said Alderton, slowly. "Actually, now that I think about it he didn't board until the second evening….."

"And how did he arrive?" asked Morecamb, incredulously. "Did he swim?"

"How the hell should I know?" thundered Alderton.

"Did you even see him coming on board?"

"Well, no. See, I was a little queasy so I went to lie down but that only made things worse. Bloody walls of the cabin started spinning so I went back up and suddenly this man appeared in front of me. I can tell you I got a fair fright. Thought I was hallucinating and he seemed surprised to see me as well. I do know there was a bit of an argument, then, but it eventually quietened down."

"And what happened after this row?"

"Well, we all sat down, had a bite to eat and a few glasses of wine…….I think I may have left then and gone to bed, or at least to the bathroom….."

There was a pause while Morecamb and Nagle, and Frahill no doubt, digested Alderton's account. Suddenly, Morecamb could see Alderton's certainty about Cuthbert begin to waver. There wasn't a hope in hell that Alderton could get out of this mess in one piece. The word, 'hallucinating' had put paid to that.

"I have to put it to you, Sergeant Alderton that this Mr Cuthbert is a figment of your imagination. There was no Mr. Cuthbert, you weren't as drunk as you claim to be and, because of a previous disagreement with Superintendent Hunter, you lost your temper, grabbed the nearest weapon, the anchor perhaps, hit him over the head and tipped him overboard. How's that for a scenario?

"Pure speculation, Inspector,"tutted Frahill. "Kindly confine yourself to questions. Do not resort to suggestions. Furthermore, where was everybody else while my client was engaged in this rather convoluted act?"

"Simple," said Morecamb, "they were in their bunks. They were the ones who were practically comatose from drink, not your client."

"Again, pure speculation. And, while we're in the land of fantasy, who, pray was piloting the boat?"

"Hunter. I presume he knew how?"

"Yes, that's true," said Alderton, "he could. Mind you, he wasn't very good but he liked to show off. I remember one time _____."

"Was he piloting the night he drowned?" asked Nagle.

"He might have been," said Alderton, excitedly. "Maybe, with the drink and all, he got careless, showing off and that, and simply fell overboard."

"And the bang on his head? How do you account for that?"

"Well, he might have banged against something on the way down," said Alderton, warming to his theme.

"But, isn't there a closed cabin where the pilot sits?" pursued Nagle.

"Well, he might have needed to relieve himself, opened the door, fell and then toppled overboard."

"Please," begged Frahill, "please don't speculate, Sergeant." Then, once again he leaned across and whispered in Alderton's ear. Alderton nodded several times and patted him on the arm.

"My Brief has advised me that I shall be responding to all future questions with a 'no comment'".

"I see," said Morecamb, "but I'm perfectly entitled to continue to ask the questions."

Frahill nodded his head in acquiescence.

"I believe you had some disagreement with Superintendent Hunter a number of years ago culminating in a complaint being made to your superiors."

"There was no complaint as you _____." Frahill tapped Alderton on the arm.

"It's okay, Ben, I've got this," said Alderton. "Hunter accused me of trying to seduce his friend's wife. Utter nonsense. The woman looked like a horse, for God's sake. But I believe that Hunter fancied her for himself and when he imagined a bit of competition from my good self, he threw a strop. Of course he knew that he wouldn't have stood a chance up against me but that's a moot point because, as I said, the woman looked like a horse _____."

"My god!" muttered Frahill. "Look, I'd like to speak to my client in private and I would appreciate an adjournment of this interview until tomorrow. I really need to speak to him," finished Frahill, mopping his brow with a fairly dishevelled looking handkerchief.

Alderton stood up abruptly, all the time glaring at Morecamb and announced, "You'll be hearing from my solicitor, Morecamb. Make no mistake about that."

As soon as the door closed behind the two men Nagle turned towards Morecamb and said, "He's fucked, isn't he?"

"Pretty much," said Morecamb. "He had motive, opportunity and has absolutely no alibi. I honestly can't see how he's going to extricate himself from this mess and the sad thing is that he has absolutely no realisation of how much trouble he's in. And he'd be an absolute car crash in the witness stand."

"I know. We'll have to charge him with murder tomorrow, Jim. I can't see any other outcome."

"Bar miracles, neither can I," said Morecamb.

Both men walked wearily towards the incident room. At least things seemed more peaceful here and even Gwen and McClean seemed to be sharing a joke. They broke off as soon as they saw Morecamb's face and the rest of the room fell silent.

"Looks like we'll be charging Sergeant Alderton with murder tomorrow," Morecamb announced.

There was a shocked silence broken by McClean, "Wow. Has he confessed?"

"Not quite," said Morecamb, "but his defence is practically non- existent. Look, we'll meet here in the morning and go over everything again. Let's say seven a.m."

*****

McClean offered Gwen a lift home but she declined. She was grateful for the offer but for the first time in a long while she felt as if she had turned a corner. The old adage, 'a problem shared is a problem halved' resonated with her. She would still carry the guilt but she felt she no longer had to skulk around. McClean, of all people, had shown her kindness and understanding and wasn't in the slightest judgemental. It reminded her that people, on the whole, were kind and each was simply getting on with their own life to the best of their ability.

She wanted to hug this new feeling of euphoria, to walk through the streets of her adopted city and feel that she belonged.

The past was simply that, the past, and it was time to move on, on equal footing with the rest of mankind.

As she stepped onto the pedestrian crossing she was oblivious to the black car swooping towards her at speed. She was tossed into the air like a rag doll and was dead before her body hit the ground.

Cuthbert felt no remorse. This was just a job and one that paid handsomely. He glanced into his rear view mirror and was satisfied that the crumpled remains of Gwen Cassidy were just that, remains.

He moved into fourth gear and headed out the Kinsale road towards Cork Airport. The hired car would be left in the airport car park, abandoned, and this time tomorrow he would be back home in London waiting for his money to come through. Mr. Big was a reliable pay-master and the two 'hits' had been delivered, as ordered. He could have no complaint.

Alright, Hunter's had been a little messy but Cassidy's was perfection itself.

He smiled at the memory.

CHAPTER 40

As soon as Morecamb entered his front door and greeted Jane he could sense her excitement.

"We are going for a scan at nine in the morning. Please tell me you'll be able to come with me".

"Of course I will," he laughed as he swung her around the kitchen. "What will we be able to see?" he asked. "Hands and feet and all that?"

"I've no idea. Certainly the heart beating, I would imagine. Oh God, at least I hope so. What if there's no heartbeat, Jim?" she asked, her face suddenly serious. "What if there's bits missing, like fingers and only a few toes? Oh my God, what if there's a body and no head?"

Suddenly the tears flowed and he spent the next ten minutes trying to console her, pointing out that her job was influencing her morbid imaginings. But every time the flow of tears started to ease she conjured up another bleak scenario.

Half an hour later they were both emotional wrecks and Morecamb suggested an early night.

"I'll just ring the duty sergeant to pass on the message that I'll be late tomorrow morning. How long do you think the scan will take?"

"I've no idea. An hour maybe? Or longer if there's something wrong. Oh my God, just imagine _____."

"You'll have to stop, Jane. You'll drive the pair of us mad and we're bad enough already as it is."

"Speak for yourself, Jim Morecamb. One of my lecturers once told me that I was the most level-headed student he had ever met," and she wailed uncontrollably for the next five minutes. Eventually, after consoling her yet again he rang the station and said he wouldn't be in the following morning until mid-day. That should give him enough time to scrape Jane up off the floor, should the occasion arise, sort out the bastard who delivered the bad news and make it to the pub on time to get a few in before resuming a day's work.

"And take the phone off the hook, please, Jim. Nothing is going to come between us and the first scan of our baby. I don't want anything to ruin this special moment. God, I can hardly wait. We'll have to leave early in the morning. If we're not there on time they might give our slot to someone else. And then we might have to wait another month before _____."

"We will not be waiting another month," Morecamb answered. "No bloody way. Another month of this doesn't bear thinking about. We'll be there on time," he yawned as he trudged up the stairs. "We'll leave here at twenty to nine."

"Twenty to nine?" she screamed, "are you mad? What if the traffic is bad? We could lose our slot _____."

"We're only a five minute drive away, for God's sake. Okay, okay," he said as he saw fresh tears glistening in her eyes, "we'll leave at eight thirty."

"Eight."

"Okay, eight it is. Now, can we go to sleep? I'm shattered."

"Me too. What about names, Jim? What do you think of Maisie, if it's a girl….."

And on it went into the night. Dawn was breaking through and Morecamb felt like crying. In fact he reckoned that he had cried himself to sleep. At seven o' clock he woke with a splitting headache and realised that Jane was already up and about and singing around the kitchen as she prepared breakfast. Morecamb didn't really feel like eating but he would prefer to lie on a bed of hot coals than admit it.

"Hungry, Jim?" asked Jane as she reached up to kiss him.

"Ravenous", he lied and grimaced as she put a full plate on the table in front of him. The rashers, sausages, eggs and black pudding were laid out in the shape of a baby and he looked at it in consternation.

"Clever, isn't it?" she asked. "Took me ages but it's good, don't you think?"

Morecamb hesitated, wondering how he was going to 'eat' said baby and on closer inspection he noticed that one of the sausages had obviously moved and there now appeared to be only one 'leg'.

For some reason he pointed out the anomaly to Jane who immediately crashed out of the kitchen in floods of tears. He hadn't the energy to follow her and simply got up and tipped his breakfast into the bin. He would settle for a cup of coffee and, as soon as he had drunk it, they would head off to the hospital. So what if they were two hours early. There was less chance of Jane getting hysterical in a crowded waiting room, hopefully. And, if there were any fireworks, he could simply leave and pretend that he wasn't with her at all. And head to the nearest pub.

"Ready?" he called up the stairs.

Jane appeared with a scowl on her face. "I don't know, do I?" she said. "What if _____."

"Christ, don't start, Jane. Everything will be fine. You're young, fit and, well…..kind of young _____."

The journey to the hospital was silent and frosty. Out of habit Morecamb indicated to turn into the General Hospital car park but a scream from Jane and frantic pointing disabused him of such a foolhardy manoeuvre and he spotted the entrance to the Maternity hospital further along. As he pulled away he noticed a squad car two cars behind him and he could have sworn that McClean was driving with Nagle in the passenger seat. But that couldn't be right. There was no way that Nagle would be sitting in the passenger seat with McClean at the helm. Looking in the rear-view mirror he saw the car indicating to pull into the General hospital.

"This is it, Jim. My God, you nearly went past it."

"Sorry but I could have sworn…..Never mind. Sleep deprivation or else I'm hallucinating."

"Well, I keep saying that you don't get enough sleep. You should go to bed earlier."

CHAPTER 41

Ever since the report of Gwen Cassidy's accident had come in, Dana-gher, the night duty sergeant had been trying to reach Morecamb.

"I think the phone is off the hook," he informed McClean who seemed to pop his head in every five minutes looking for an update. And, when at 6am, the news filtered through that Gwen was declared dead, all hell had broken loose.

Nagle had contacted Thornhill with the news, which was greeted with silence. O' Sullivan and Lewis were sent to Morecamb's house to tell him and McClean had forcibly shaken himself out of his stupor and sent out an alert to other divisions to be on the look-out for a black Mercedes seen speeding from the scene. The witness to the hit and run had been a visitor to the country and was unfamiliar with the city but was sure that it had gone 'that way', a route which would have abruptly dispatched the offending car straight into the River Lee.

McClean wanted the witness arrested until she came to her senses but Nagle vetoed the suggestion, recognising the glint of desperation in McClean's eyes.

"Let's head out to the hospital, sergeant," said Nagle. "We need to speak to the doctors who worked on Gwen and get details of her injuries. Okay? And you can drive," he added as he gave the keys to McClean. He hoped that this might help the sergeant to stay focussed though he knew that he would probably come to regret the offer.

"I don't know your Christian name, Sergeant," said Nagle as they headed towards the hospital. "Mine is Liam."

McClean hesitated for a moment and then said quietly, "It's Alphonsus."

"Ah. A good, strong name," said Nagle though he secretly believed that McClean's mother should be battered for inflicting a name like that on her son. "Is it okay if I call you, Al?"

"Yes, please do," said McClean and he heaved a sigh of relief, remembering the various permutations of the name when he had been a school boy, all of them derogatory and possibly even slanderous.

They drove to the hospital in silence. McClean didn't know which emotion dominated, sadness or anger. How could somebody knock down a woman and leave her lying on the road, dying? You wouldn't do it to a dog, for Christ's sake.

He was glad that he hadn't seen Gwen before the ambulance had rushed her to the hospital. He wondered if she had been in pain. Did she know that she was dying? Or was she already dead at that stage? He hoped to God that she had, at least, been unconscious. And he resolved, as he ran a red light, that he would throttle the bastard who had done it with his bare hands.

The question was would they be able to find him? They weren't even sure which route he had taken. He could be anywhere.

McClean was also faced with another dilemma. Should he confide in Morecamb and tell him about Gwen's association with Hunter? Strictly speaking he wouldn't be breaking a confidence as Gwen hadn't exactly confided in him. But she had left him in no doubt either. And she did mention that she had lost the baby. My God, what did the poor woman ever do to deserve _____."

"Maybe you should slow down a little, Al?" said Nagle as he stared open-mouthed at the speedometer. It didn't matter who you were if the traffic cops saw you driving at eighty miles per hour in a thirty mile zone. "Anyhow, we're here now," continued Nagle, "you can park over there."

McClean didn't seem to hear him and parked directly in front of the A&E, in a space reserved for ambulances. They'd be lucky if the car was still there when they returned.

*****

"Ah, here we are," said the Sonographer as she moved the scanner over Jane's stomach and turned the monitor towards them. "See that?"

Morecamb could see nothing except some grainy images. Certainly nothing that looked like his fry-up earlier that morning. But he kept his reservations to himself.

"See that?" she continued, "there's the head."

Jane raised herself a little from the pillow and nodded excitedly. "Yes, yes, I can see it," she practically shouted.

"Actually," the Sonographer paused, "I can see a second head."

Morecamb felt the floor rising to meet him and his next conscious memory was of sitting in a chair and Jane babbling, "We're having twins, Jim. Twins. Oh my God, I can't believe it!"

"Drink the water, Mr Morecamb," ordered the nurse, who had obviously been summoned. "Every last drop," she admonished with her hands on her hips, glaring at him. Then she turned to Jane and they had a lengthy discussion on the weaknesses and frailties of the male of the species and perhaps it might be best if Jane left her husband outside the door for the delivery.

Later, in the car as Morecamb turned the ignition, Jane asked him if he had counted the fingers and toes.

"I didn't see any," he croaked. "Just the two heads."

CHAPTER 42

Danagher almost rugby tackled him as he came through the door of the station. He had dropped Jane off at the mortuary and had carried on in a daze.

"Where have you been, Inspector?" demanded Danagher.

The cheek of the man, thought Morecamb.

"We've been looking everywhere for you all morning," and he went on to tell him about Gwen.

On hearing the news Morecamb was afraid that he was going to hit the floor for a second time that morning. And, once again, he could hardly believe what he was hearing.

Just as Danagher had finished his report McClean and Nagle arrived, ashen-faced.

"We've just come back from the hospital, Jim."

"Christ, I can't believe it," said Morecamb. "When did it happen? And where?"

"She had just left the station last night and was knocked down at the pedestrian crossing opposite McDade's pub."

"I had offered her a lift home," added McClean with a tremor in his voice, "but she said….."

His voice tailed off.

"She had multiple injuries," continued Nagle. "There was nothing the doctors could do."

"And nothing on the driver?" asked Morecamb.

"We've put out an alert to all stations but nothing so far."

"Let's have a meeting in the Incident Room. Is the Superintendent in yet, Danagher?"

"Yes, sir, she arrived about five minutes ago and went straight into her office. And Lewis and Sullivan are back as well."

"Right, let's get started," ordered Morecamb. "We have two enquiries to conduct now. We'll need re-enforcements. McClean, will you ask the Superintendent to join us?"

"Inspector, could I have a word first, please," asked McClean. "It might be important _____."

"No, it will have to wait. Now, go. Come on, Nagle."

"Morecamb!" The familiar figure of Alderton rounded the corner and barrelled down the corridor towards him. "What the hell is going on?"

"Not now, Alderton."

"I'm entitled to know what the hell is going on," snapped Alderton. "Is it true that one of my officers was mown down in a hit and run? Plus, I need to run something by you."

"Yes, Sergeant Cassidy was the victim of a hit and run but you shouldn't be here. Go down to the Cold Cases' unit. Of course you shouldn't be down there either but I simply don't have the time to deal with you right now."

"I'll wait for you in your office, Morecamb. I'll give you ten minutes."

"Can you believe that man?" asked Morecamb turning towards Nagle. "In any other station he would be locked up at this stage."

"Is everything okay with you, Jim? We've been trying all morning to get in touch with you."

"Yes, sorry about that. I'll explain later. Maybe you could ask Danagher and Moloney to join us. We'll need all hands on deck. Sullivan," he called across the room, "will you go and fetch Murphy up here. He should be down in the Cold Cases' unit."

Five minutes later they were all assembled, except Thornhill who, according to McClean, would be joining them shortly.

The mood in the room was sombre, each man lost in his own thoughts. The absence of Gwen was almost tangible and, though her time at the station had been brief, nevertheless they were all conscious of the empty chair.

"Okay, folks, let's get started. Two enquiries, two victims and each deserves our utmost commitment in seeking justice for them. I know that your anger will, no doubt, put Gwen's murder to the forefront of your mind but, as I said, both deserve closure so I'm going to divide the team into two."

There was a pause as Thornhill entered and, instead of taking her customary spot at the top of the room, she chose to sit at the back. Her face was etched in stone and she stared straight ahead, acknowledging nobody.

Morecamb carried on. "Detective Nagle, I want you to lead the Hunter enquiry and I'll head up the investigation into Gwen's death.

"Obviously, Sergeant Alderton is our only suspect," he continued, "for the murder of Hunter. You might notice that I didn't say the 'obvious' suspect because I'm still not sure of his involvement. So, in the absence of probability we're left with possibility….a poor substitute, I know. But, go back over all the statements again and look for any anomaly whatsoever.

As I said, I'm leading on Gwen's murder and, so far, we're working in the dark. But our main priority is locating that black Mercedes. So, let's get to work and let's solve these crimes."

As he looked around the room he noticed that Thornhill had already left. She hadn't uttered a word, had shown no inclination to become involved and had made no offer to strengthen the crew with extra men. What a cold bloody fish! The sooner they got rid of her, the better. He would personally escort her to the airport with her bag and baggage.

He bent down to gather his papers and when he straightened up McClean had materialised in front of him.

"Can I speak to you now, sir? You said _____."

"Not just yet, McClean. I have Sergeant Alderton in my office and I need to get rid of him first. Then you can come in."

Alderton jumped up out of his seat as soon as Morecamb entered his office. He immediately began a tirade about the boorish behaviour in the senior ranks and what else could one expect from the likes of Murphy when he had been nurtured on the flotsam which swirled around every corner and which had deteriorated in a marked fashion since the most heinous grievance had been perpetrated against his good self.

"Shut up, Alderton and get to the point."

Alderton resumed his seat, his puff spent after his rant and he seemed to shrink a little, his hands hanging loosely between his knees and his face creased with lines and furrows which seemed to have appeared almost overnight.

"Look, Morecamb, I'm sorry about Sergeant Cassidy. I know I wasn't very nice or indeed welcoming towards her. And I regret that. But I don't believe that the Garda force is the right place for a woman. Maybe I'm a bit of a dinosaur _____."

"Well, you don't have any objections to Superintendent Thornhill."

"Well…..that's different. But, you're right. I suppose that makes me a hypocrite in your eyes but….where is she, by the way?"

"Who?"

"Superintendent Thornhill."

"In her office, I presume."

"No, her door is locked and she is always glad to see me and _____."

"Alderton, why are we having this discussion? You said you need-ed to see me and if this is the extent of your concerns in the middle of _____."

"No, no, as I said earlier, I just wanted to run something by you. As the days go on I seem to be remembering more about that fatal trip. Remember, I told you about the fact that there actually were two toilets _____."

"Oh my God, Alderton, I'm going to throw you out the window."

"Yes, well, I've remembered something else. I think. It was Detective Nagle who triggered it, actually. He mentioned a man called Drummond and I couldn't remember when I had heard the name recently. And then it came to me. I remembered that Cuthbert man talking to Superintendent Wallace and they seemed to be having an argument and Cuthbert definitely mentioned Drummond's name."

You could hear a pin drop in the room. Morecamb felt the blood drain from his face and he loosened his tie in an effort to harness as much air as possible and force it into his lungs. He gripped the edge of the table for support.

Both men looked at each other in silence, Morecamb grappling with an unpleasant realisation and Alderton wondering if he had somehow, unwittingly, grabbed a life-line.

"Are you sure?" Morecamb asked eventually.

"As sure as I can be. Why else did the name of a man that I've never heard of or met resonate with me?"

"Okay, come with me."

"Where am I going?"

"I want you to repeat what you've just told me to Detective Nagle."

As Morecamb hurriedly threw open the door he saw McClean pacing up and down the corridor.

"McClean," he said, "we'll have to postpone our _____."

"No, sir." Morecamb stopped but McClean stood his ground. He could hear Alderton tut tutting beside him.

"I need to speak with you, sir."

"Right, right," he acknowledged impatiently. "Alderton, wait there and don't move from that spot. If you do _____."

"Don't worry, Morecamb, I shall obey. After all, in view of my earlier observations on the escalating lack of respect in evidence since my removal from my rightful position......."

Morecamb left him talking to an empty corridor and beckoned McClean into his office.

"Okay, McClean, let's hear it," said Morecamb, going over to open the window as far as it would go. Then he came back and stood in front of McClean.

"Sir, Sergeant Gwen Cassidy was having an affair with the late Superintendent Hunter."

There! He'd said it. He could feel rivers of perspiration flowing down his back. For a moment he felt consumed with guilt and he wished Morecamb would say something, anything. But his boss was rendered speechless, wondering if he was still in bed and the morning's events and revelations were simply a nightmare. Well, several nightmares.

"Sir?" prompted McClean.

Morecamb visibly shook himself out of his reverie.

"Who told you that?" he asked quietly.

"Well, initially, Hunter's sister mentioned that he had been having an affair with a fellow officer. Obviously, I use the term 'fellow officer' loosely as it was definitely a woman and she became pregnant."

For once Morecamb didn't interrupt McClean. He just stared at him, open-mouthed so McClean continued.

"Gwen seemed very agitated after my phone call with Hunter's sister and demanded to know what she had said. I told her and when I mentioned the rumour of the pregnancy she admitted that she had lost the baby."

"My God."

"Exactly, sir. And now I'm wondering if her death could be somehow connected with, you know……" McClean hesitated to finish the sentence. The connection had simply seemed too far-fetched to articulate.

Morecamb just stood still, staring at McClean in disbelief, much as he had been rendered speechless by Alderton's revelation.

My God, he wondered, is it possible that the two greatest twits in the whole station each held a key to unlocking this labyrinth. Suddenly he sprang into action and told McClean to fetch Nagle and "ask Alderton to wait in interview room one and I'll be with him shortly."

CHAPTER 43

As Morecamb relayed the latest revelations to Nagle he could see his own range of emotions reflected in the detective's expressions.

"You know what this means, Nagle?"

"Yes. The two enquiries become one."

"Do you remember what Lonergan said at the end of our interrogation of him? He hinted that someone in the force called the final shots in that Company he's involved in."

"I remember. He called him Mr. Big."

"Yes, and if I remember correctly he said that Mr. Big joined the force around the same time as he did, a little later in fact."

"And now we have your friend Drummond thrown into the mix."

Both men started pacing the confined dimensions of Morecamb's office. To the casual observer it looked like some crazy dance, each circling in opposite directions and performing a kind of jagged pirouette when they looked like colliding with each other.

"We need to think hard about this, Nagle, we need a strategy. Let's sit down and map it out. The first thing we need to decide is who we can trust."

They made a list. Wallace, Drummond, Lonergan and his sister all joined the group of suspects.

"What about Thornhill?" asked Nagle.

"For the moment she's in that group too," and he reached for his pen and scrawled her name at the bottom.

"You know, in the beginning of the enquiry she was certainly no fan of either Lonergan or Wallace and she got very angsty when we were questioning Alderton," said Nagle thinking out loud.

"Yes, she practically accused me of trying to shoe-horn him into the role of murderer," added Morecamb.

"But that changed didn't it? In the next breath she was practically insisting that Alderton was our man."

"So, obviously someone got to her in the meantime because I don't think she would have changed so dramatically unless someone was cracking the whip," said Morecamb, getting up and starting to pace again.

After several minutes of back and forth they decided that the man who was the puppeteer was this Mr. Big and the most likely candidate for that role was Drummond. Morecamb, once again, experienced the twin jolts of disappointment and anger.

"Christ, I can't believe it," he muttered.

"Hiding in plain sight, Jim. It's how the best of them operate. What about Alderton?"

"You know, I think Alderton is key. He identified the Cuthbert man who, I believe, was brought on board to specifically get rid of Hunter. But why kill Hunter? Oh, God, we're going around in bloody circles. Will you ask Sullivan to fetch a few coffees for us?"

As Nagle stepped out he spotted an irate Alderton heading in his direction.

"Out of my way, please," he snapped and pushed his way past Nagle.

"Morecamb, this is more of it. I've been _____."

"Sit down, Alderton. Nagle," he called, "make that three coffees, will you?"

"What's going on, Morecamb?"

"I'll explain in a minute. Just wait until Nagle gets back."

Morecamb had decided, almost on a whim, to take Alderton into their confidence. He'd never truly believed that he was in the frame for the murder and if Thornhill had been colluding with those involved, then her eagerness to point the finger at Alderton, had, perversely, put him in the clear.

Nagle frowned in Alderton's direction when he returned but Morecamb nodded his head slightly. Almost immediately Sullivan arrived with the coffees on a tray and put it down in front of Morecamb.

"I don't drink coffee," pouted Alderton.

"Well, you will now. Thanks, Sullivan."

As soon as the door closed Morecamb filled Alderton in on their conclusions so far and, for once, he didn't interrupt. At the end, having finished his coffee, he gently placed his cup back on the tray and uttered his first sensible sentence in living memory.

"You don't have any proof, Morecamb," he said.

"That's true," he admitted grudgingly. "But we have to find proof."

"What about Commissioner O' Toole, Jim? I remember you telling me on the way back from Dublin that he seemed to be nervous around Drummond. Is it possible that he's not in the inner circle?"

"Mmmm, hard to know but we desperately need someone we can trust up there."

"I remember O' Toole," volunteered Alderton. "I worked with him briefly at H.Q."

"How did you find him?"

"Well, he was a stickler for the rules. Everything had to be written out in triplicate. A right pain in the ass. I couldn't stand the man, if I'm honest. And that is certainly a black mark against the man because, as you know, I have always been on the best of terms with my colleagues. In fact I was voted the _____."

"You'll have to stop there. Tell us about your relationship with Superintendent Thornhill."

"Well, that's private, isn't it? A gentleman never divulges _____."

"Have you any idea of the predicament you're in right now?" Morecamb hissed. "The Superintendent wants you charged with murder, Wallace and Lonergan are definitely pointing the finger at you and Sergeant Cassidy is dead because, in all probability, someone believed that she knew something incriminating. So, that just leaves you."

"It might be an idea to arrange some protection for Sergeant Alderton, Jim."

"But I don't know anything!" thundered Alderton. "The Superintendent didn't tell me anything. In fact she was very reticent to discuss anything of a private nature with me and certainly nothing relating to Hunter's death."

Suddenly he jolted forward in his seat. "Protection?" he gasped. "What did you mean by protection? Good God, am I in danger? What kind of shit-show have you landed us in, Morecamb? I shall hold you personally if there's the slightest threat to my person."

"You may not be a target," said Morecamb crossly. "I think their plan for you is a life time in jail for murder."

"Oh, that's alright then, isn't it?" roared Alderton, rising out of his seat. "Have you any idea how members of the force are treated by the other inmates in prison?"

"It won't come to that," said Nagle. "We just need to find proof."

"And what about my wife?" said Alderton, starting to rise again. "She could be a target as well, mown down like poor Sergeant Cassidy and left for dead……" Suddenly he stopped and quickly ran through the ramifications of that scenario in his head.

The other two men were looking at him expectantly, waiting for him to continue. When there was no sign of him adding anything further Morecamb spoke.

"I think we need to bring O' Toole on board. It's a risk, I know but from what you just said about him, Alderton, and the obvious antipathy which he displayed towards Drummond I think we have to trust him. What do you think?"

"I agree," Nagle said, "but I don't think we should tell him everything just yet. Sound him out first on Drummond. See what he says."

"Yes, I'll give him a ring. Maybe we should go out and have some lunch first. Clear the head. Alderton, you're coming with us. We'll be your protection for today."

"I presume that's meant to be a joke," said Morecamb, sourly. "What about Superintendent Thornhill? I'll just go along and ask her to join us. She and I always _____."

"Alderton, have you been listening to a word we've said?" bellowed Morecamb. "See what I have to put up with, Nagle?"

CHAPTER 44

After a quick lunch, for which none of them had much of an appetite, the three men returned to the station. Morecamb went straight into his office and Nagle brought Alderton into the Incident Room with strict instructions to stay out of the way.

He got through to O' Toole straight away and didn't bother with any preliminaries.

"We have a situation here, Commissioner and I need your word that none of what I'm about to tell you will go further than us."

"This sounds very ominous, Inspector, but, please continue."

"Do I have your word?"

"Yes, yes, of course."

He decided to tell him everything. At least, if there was a leak, then he would know the source without any doubts.

When he was finished there was silence at the other end of the phone. Morecamb held his breath, knowing that the next few minutes would reveal the wisdom or otherwise of confiding in O' Toole.

"I'll ring you back in about ten minutes," was all O' Toole said.

Morecamb replaced the phone and cursed himself. Oh, my God, he muttered, what have I done? Slowly he rose from his desk and went to consult Nagle. When he entered the Incident Room he noticed that Alderton seemed occupied, admonishing Lewis about his poor spelling and the disgraceful state of his desk.

Morecamb beckoned Nagle aside and filled him in on his conversation with O' Toole. Nagle listened to him in silence and then said, "We had no other choice, Jim. As things stood we were completely stagnant and it is impossible to move this enquiry forward without some sort of access to the main players. And for that, we need an ally in H.Q. and O' Toole is our best shot."

"True, but we might have to come up with a Plan B and pretty quickly. Well, let's see how this pans out first. Let's see which side O' Toole is on. How's Alderton behaving, by the way?"

"He's not."

In spite of himself Morecamb smiled as he left the room. In the midst of chaos some things never changed, he mused and Alderton and his whimsies were a constant. There was a perverse kind of comfort in the knowledge.

He had just reached the door of his office when the phone rang. He hurriedly snatched it up.

This time it was O' Toole who didn't bother with the preliminaries.

"I'm ringing from an outside phone," he began. "I'm not too sure about the security of the internal lines. I've long held the suspicion that…..well, never mind. Your accusations are fairly startling, to say the least but you obviously don't have any definitive proof."

"True, but _____."

"I think you need to take out the minnows first, so to speak," continued O' Toole, as if Morecamb hadn't spoken. "Let's assume for the moment that Drummond is the king pin. I think our best option is to target Lonergan and Wallace."

Morecamb felt a great weight lift from his shoulders. When O' Toole mentioned the word 'we', he knew that they had an ally in H.Q. Of course it could be just a ruse but he had committed himself now and there was no going back. "Yes," said Morecamb, "I had the same thought."

"We need to ambush them, so to speak, as quickly as we can, but, we can't alert Drummond. Let me think……..actually, Drummond is away for a day or two. I'm not sure where he's gone but I've been told the usual; meetings, committees and such. He seems to attend a lot of those. Here's what I suggest. You come to Dublin first thing in the morning.

Come straight to my office and you and I will interview Wallace and Lonergan. Obviously don't mention anything to Thornhill."

Morecamb had a sick feeling in his stomach. Had he gone straight into the lion's den? Maybe he was the one who was going to be ambushed and all he had in his defence was speculation and, oh my God, Alderton as his main witness.

"Bring one or two of your own men with you as they will need to 'babysit' one of our suspects while we interview the other. I'll see you at nine."

Morecamb could feel his heart racing as he slowly replaced the phone. He sat for a moment or two contemplating the end of his career. He didn't know how he was going to tell Jane. The shock might precipitate a miscarriage. He couldn't do that. He couldn't tell her. But how could he hide it? Leave the house every morning and pretend he was going into work? And how long would that last? One phone call from Pathology, asking for him and the proverbial would hit the fan. God, what a bloody mess.

He went back to the Incident Room and called the team together. He would have to carry on as normal though he knew that Nagle would suspect something was wrong. He would explain later.

Alderton would have to stay in the room for the briefing as he couldn't be trusted anywhere else, especially on his own.

Morecamb relayed the news about the merging of the two enquiries. At first they were shocked but then they became animated and seemed imbued with renewed determination. He thanked McClean and Alderton for their huge contribution.

"And so you should," huffed Alderton, loudly.

Meanwhile, McClean thought he'd died and gone to heaven and when Morecamb further announced that McClean would be travelling to Dublin with himself and Nagle the following morning, well, he thought he might have to excuse himself and do a dance in the men's toilets.

"Now", continued Morecamb, "in view of your help, Sergeant Alderton, I'm putting you in a cell overnight in order to guarantee your personal safety."

He didn't wait for the explosion but instead called for a round of applause for McClean and Alderton. As he had hoped the applause was raucous and drowned out the ranting and swearing from Alderton. He was almost apoplectic by the time it ended.

Sergeant McClean excused himself and left the room.

When things had calmed a little Alderton strutted to the top of the room and planted himself in front of Morecamb.

"I shall be suing of course," he began, "you realise that, don't you? Oh yes, have no doubt. But, as usual, my own concerns are secondary at the moment because I'm worried about Superintendent Thornhill. I haven't seen her all day which is quite unusual."

"So what do you want me to do? You said yourself that her door is locked. Or are you suggesting that we should break it down?"

CHAPTER 45

The suicide note was addressed to Alderton.

Instead of using a battering ram on Thornhill's door, Lewis had, worryingly, proved quite adept at picking the lock. When they went inside they found the Superintendent slumped over her desk, two empty pill bottles in front of her.

Alderton had to be restrained in his grief and blamed Morecamb for the whole thing. Nagle was glad that she hadn't used her gun. But of course, in that case, they would have heard the shot and perhaps got to her sooner. Either way it was a sorry sight and, while she hadn't endeared herself to the team, nevertheless an air of despondency seemed to descend.

Morecamb donned protective gloves, picked up the note and then ordered the whole area to be cordoned off. Nagle rang for a doctor and an ambulance, not in any expectation that the victim could be revived. He reckoned she had been dead for two or three hours at least, judging by the waxen hue of her face.

While they waited for the paramedics Morecamb telephoned O' Toole and gave him the news. The man seemed to be in a state of shock. Probably wondering if he should send in the army, Morecamb thought. When he went back to the others he gave the note to Alderton and ordered him to open it and tell them what it said. Alderton hesitated at first, but then, with shaking hands he ripped open the seal. He read it through, silently, and then handed it to Morecamb.

Morecamb skimmed through it and then read it aloud.

My dear William, please don't judge me harshly. I feel I have no other option. A life of ignominy or, worse, incarceration, doesn't really appeal to me. I'm afraid I've been stupid.

I left the States under a cloud, shall we say, and I can't go back.

A few days ago I had a phone call from one of our number in Dublin. He delivered an ultimatum. If I did all in my power to incriminate your good self in the murder of Superintendent Hunter and didn't reveal that there was indeed a man named Cuthbert on board, then he wouldn't reveal my past.

I knew I couldn't risk that and I'm ashamed to say that I acquiesced.

You are a good man and I have enjoyed your excellent and sophisticated company. You were an oasis in a cultural wasteland…. "Bloody bitch", intoned Morecamb……With a heavy heart I now sign off,

Your affectionate friend, Caroline.

"Is that it?" queried Morecamb. "No identification of the individual who made that call to her? Well, that's a huge help, isn't it?" he raged, still smarting at the remark she made about everyone else at the station. "The least she could have done was given us some bloody lead. What harm would it have done? She's dead now anyway," he added as he threw the letter aside.

"Well, I hardly think that's Caroline's fault, do you?" asked Alderton, equally angry.

Morecamb stared at him, dumbfounded.

"Will somebody speak to that man, please? I'm going to my office."

Half an hour later Thornhill's body was removed to the mortuary and a team of Crime Scene personnel descended on her office. Alderton was duly escorted to a cell, in spite of his protestations that he was a man in mourning and Morecamb dismissed the team.

"We'll gather here at six in the morning. I'll assign you your duties and then Nagle, McClean and myself will head to Dublin".

Before he left the station Morecamb rang O' Toole and told him about Thornhill's suicide note. For the next ten minutes they discussed the situation and agreed that Drummond was the most likely candidate for the mysterious call to Thornhill.

*****

It was late when he got home. A small table lamp was lit in the empty living room. He tip-toed up to the bedroom, hoping that he wouldn't waken Jane. But he needn't have worried. She was sitting up in bed, wide awake.

"I heard about Gwen, Jim. I'm so sorry. How are you? I was wondering why I hadn't heard from you all day."

"Look, Jane," pleaded Morecamb as he lay down, fully clothed, on the bed.

"Oh, it's not a criticism," she added hastily, "I was just worried about you when I heard about Gwen. You must have been devastated when you heard the news."

"Yes, the whole station is and that's only the half of it." He went on to tell her about Gwen's relationship with Hunter and their suspicion that the two deaths were linked. Strictly speaking he shouldn't be telling her at all but, with a jolt he realised, that there was no one else that he trusted so completely.

He put his arm around her shoulder and drew her towards him.

"I love you, Jane," he said.

"I know," she smiled, looking up at him, "I've known for a long time. I was just waiting for you to catch up!"

He laughed, amazed that he still had the capacity.

"On a serious note," she continued, "I'll be doing the Post Mortem on Gwen tomorrow. Will you be there?"

"I'm afraid not," he replied and went on to tell her about Superintendent Thornhill.

"Oh no, that is so awful. Poor woman."

It suddenly dawned on her that she would be carrying out two Post Mortems the following day and Jim wouldn't be at either. Her heart sank.

"Two babies, two bodies," she whispered as the tears threatened to flow.

"I know," he said. "Life is a bitch. Do you think you'll find the whole process more difficult now?"

"Yes, without a doubt. You know, I was thinking today that I'm starting to dread the whole dissecting of bodies and that was before I even heard about Gwen. Maybe I could step aside, for a while at least. But I honestly don't know if I'll feel any differently when we have our two little babies. The beginning of life and the ending of life all on the same day." And this time the tears did flow and Morecamb held her tightly.

"If you want to give up, Jane, then do. We'll manage."

He decided not to tell her about the nightmare of possibly losing his job and being black-listed from ever again securing a place on the force.

He'd know tomorrow.

CHAPTER 46

Moloney was under strict instructions to keep an eye on Alderton in the cell. Meanwhile, the others were to divvy up the two Post Mortems among them and write up the findings. In the event of the report from the Scene of Crime officers arriving before Morecamb got back from Dublin they could just put it on his desk in his office.

Morecamb, McClean and Nagle arrived at H.Q. at nine on the dot. It had been a strange journey, each man conscious of the enormity of the task ahead, each knowing that they could be making the return journey in their civvies.

They were ushered straight up to the second floor and O' Toole appeared at his door and greeted them quietly.

"Once again, my condolences to you all on the death of Sergeant Cassidy. And now, of course, the death of Superintendent Thornhill though, obviously, in different circumstances. Let's see if we can start the journey of getting justice for Sergeant Cassidy. And indeed for Superintendent Hunter. Sit down. Tea or coffee, anyone?"

They all declined, wanting to get proceedings underway before they went over the edge from nerves.

O' Toole got straight to the point.

"I'll have both men brought up straight away. I've managed to secure the services of two solicitors. We don't want some judge telling us that procedure wasn't followed and the evidence declared inadmissible. We'll start with Lonergan, because, if your hunch is correct, Inspector, he is the one who is most closely associated with the possible genesis of all this."

"Yes," agreed Morecamb. "I also get the impression that he is the more likely to crack."

"Good. Give me a minute, will you? I'll be back shortly."

He got up, walked out and closed the door softly behind him.

"Oh, Christ, what now!" exclaimed Nagle. His palms started to sweat and suddenly Portlaoise seemed like an oasis of calm. If he came out of this intact he would ask for an immediate transfer and head back, wife or no wife.

McClean forlornly remembered his school days and the jeers and jibes. This uniform had given him an element of gravitas, an ability to walk the streets of Cork with his head held high. Of course he might still end up on the streets as a lowly garda, being called upon to sort out the usual quota of Saturday night brawls and domestics. The one upside, he thought, was the possibility that those bullies of yore were probably still the same and had now taken to beating up on their fellow citizens.

If that was the case he would enjoy giving some of them a good thumping, whether warranted or not. His racing heart eased as he resolved to enrol in a gym as soon as he got back to Cork.

"Maybe we should have brought a solicitor with us, lads," said Morecamb. "If this goes tits- up we might be joining Alderton. I don't think I could live with that."

He could just imagine the smug, 'I told you', look on his face. It would be unbearable. Suddenly Jane's face swam into view as she digested the news. He quickly dispelled it, grateful for the appearance of O' Toole with Lonergan and a stranger in tow.

"This is Mr. Evans, Inspector Lonergan's solicitor," said O' Toole, by way of introduction. "You already know his client."

Lonergan did a double take when he saw Morecamb and looked at O' Toole.

"These men would like to put a few questions to you, Inspector. But, first, you'll have to excuse Detective Nagle and Sergeant McClean. Will you come with me, gentlemen?"

As soon as they left the silent room behind O' Toole clamped a hand on Nagle's shoulder.

"Don't look so worried. We'll sort this out. I'm taking you to the room where Superintendent Wallace is conferring with his solicitor. Just stay in the vicinity and make sure that our suspect doesn't leave. Accompany him to the gents if he needs to go. I'll get coffee and hopefully a few biscuits sent over to you."

As he turned to go Nagle and McClean looked at each other.

"Do you think a last cigarette is still offered to a man as he faces the firing squad, Al?" said Nagle, in an attempt to ease the tension.

"I don't smoke," said McClean, "though I could always start."

*****

The room was still silent when O' Toole returned to it. Morecamb was over by the window, with his back to the other two occupants and was staring out onto the courtyard.

"Commissioner O' Toole, we'd appreciate if you could get on with this business." Evans was obviously determined to control proceedings. "I'm sure we all have better things to do than sit around here twiddling our thumbs, so to speak."

"Of course. I do apologise. Let's get started."

Morecamb grabbed a chair and brought it over beside O' Toole so that both sets of men now sat facing each other.

"Inspector Lonergan," began O' Toole, "you've already been questioned under caution but some new evidence has come to light regarding the events in Kinsale. We'll be interviewing Superintendent Wallace straight after this and we'll be putting the same questions to him."

Lonergan seemed to pale a little and, at this last statement, looked to his solicitor as if for guidance.

"What so..sort of information?" Lonergan stammered.

"Well, we have now established that there was a Mr. Cuthbert on board the night of Inspector Hunter's death. So, would you like to revise your original statement?"

"My client won't be making any comment on that until I have conferred with him."

"Let's try another question then, shall we? How complicit were you in the death of Sergeant Gwen Cassidy?"

"Once again, my client won't be making a comment."

"I can answer that," croaked Lonergan. "I had absolutely no involvement whatsoever in that."

"Glad to hear it. So, let's revisit the question of Mr Cuthbert and see if you can be equally adamant about that."

"No comment."

"You realise that by failing to cooperate, Inspector, you are only increasing our suspicions," Morecamb put in.

"Please do not attempt to bully my client."

"Regarding your family company," O' Toole ploughed on, "can you tell us more about the sort of merchandise which you carry, apart from the tea, coffee and, olive oil, I believe?"

"No comment."

"We believe your sister has the largest share in the Company but there is also, shall we say, a silent partner. Can you tell us who he is?"

"No comment."

O' Toole turned to Morecamb and suggested that it would be a good idea to give the Inspector some time to think about his predicament and confer with his solicitor. "And, in the meantime, we will question Superintendent Wallace and see if he can enlighten us any further. Wait here, Inspector and please do not leave my office."

Lonergan, if possible, went a whiter shade of pale and stared intently at his nails. He didn't even raise his eyes to acknowledge their departure.

"What do you think, Morecamb?" O' Toole asked as the door closed behind them.

"Hard to know. Our best bet is that he'll be afraid of what Wallace tells us and lands Lonergan in the proverbial. But I don't think Wallace will tell us anything but Lonergan won't know that."

"True. Let's play one off against the other."

McClean and Nagle were relieved when they saw the two men coming towards them, especially as their boss looked unscathed.

"Any attempt from Wallace to bolt?"

"No, Commissioner, all quiet," Nagle responded.

"Right, I've another job for you. Same thing, stand guard outside my office now and make sure that Inspector Lonergan doesn't make a run for it. I've given him strict instructions to stay where he is."

*****

Lonergan was shaking as he heard the door click closed behind. He put his head in his hands and when Evans asked if he was okay he simply said, "No comment."

Evans decided that the whole force should be disbanded forthwith. The current lot, from what he could see, seemed to be a bunch of imbeciles. He got up and went over to the window, taking up an almost identical position as the one previously occupied by Morecamb, ignoring his client in the process.

Meanwhile his client felt he was staring down the barrel of disaster. For the first time in his life he had found love and he desperately wanted to hold on to it. But it seemed that, with every twist and turn in his life, fate was conspiring against him. He suddenly felt an impotent rage and knew that if Evans hadn't been there he would simply have ended it all. But then the image of his lover's face came to mind and he knew he would do whatever it took to protect him.

CHAPTER 47

Wallace was exhibiting no signs of nerves. He sat back scowling at his inquisitors and Morecamb could almost predict a volley of "No comments" to every question.

O' Toole made the introductions.

"This is Mr. O' Gorman, Wallace's barrister and this is Detective Inspector Morecamb". Both men nodded to each other and then Morecamb started the tape.

"We've just had an interesting conversation with Inspector Lonergan," O' Toole began, "and we'd like to hear your version of events now."

Morecamb marvelled at O' Toole's choice of words. The innuendo was unmistakable but he couldn't be accused of lying.

"Let's start with Mr. Cuthbert."

"No comment," said Wallace stifling a yawn.

"I haven't asked you a question yet, Superintendent. Were you aware of an altercation between Superintendent Hunter and Mr. Cuthbert?"

Morecamb, who had been watching Wallace intently, detected a narrowing of his eyes and a slight tremor in one of his hands.

"Can you answer the question, please, Superintendent?"

"No comment."

"Were you aware that this man Cuthbert would be joining you on the second day of the trip?" asked Morecamb, remembering Alderton's rather frayed memory. Still, there was no harm in throwing it out there. Wallace wouldn't know where the information had come from. He might even blame Lonergan for the revelation.

"No comment."

And so it continued for the next twenty minutes. Wallace continued to stonewall them though he was far less comfortable by the time Morecamb turned off the tape and O' Toole asked both men to remain where they were.

"What now?" Morecamb asked as soon as they left the room.

"I'm going to apply to the Court to have both men detained for a further twenty four hours. I don't seriously believe that either man is going to change his approach but if they continue with this no comment business I suggest we charge them with the murder of Hunter."

"But what about Cuthbert?" Morecamb asked beginning to feel a little uncomfortable at the sudden turn of events.

"Well, you heard both men deny that Cuthbert was on board. Your friend, Alderton was, by all accounts, practically comatose so, that leaves our two friends here. The only other person who could have done it was this Cuthbert man but both of them deny he was ever there. So, by a process of elimination........."

Morecamb felt he was backed into a corner. Much as he disliked Lonergan and Wallace and suspected their involvement in the rather shady business of that shipping company he still didn't have them pegged for Hunter's murder.

"We'll take it from here, Inspector Morecamb. We probably should have investigated Hunter's murder here in H.Q. from the beginning _____."

"Look, Commissioner," Morecamb interrupted, "I'm not happy with this _____."

"And neither am I," O' Toole retorted. "How do you think I feel having to charge two fine, long-serving officers from my Department and the murder of a very decent man."

Morecamb could feel his anger beginning to boil over.

"Sergeant Gwen Cassidy would put all those men in the bloody shade _____."

"Sergeant Cassidy behaved abominably before she had to be transferred," said an equally angry O' Toole. "As for Thornhill, the only reason she replaced Alderton was out of necessity. Nobody else was interested in a transfer so who were we going to put in his place? You?"

Nagle had spotted the confrontation between the two men and decided it might be prudent to intervene. As he neared them he called out, "Commissioner O' Toole, Inspector Lonergan has asked several times to go to the bathroom." He hadn't but it was the only excuse that Nagle could come up with at short notice.

His intervention had the desired effect and both men, visibly, took a step backwards.

"Thank you, Sergeant _____."

"It's *Detective* Nagle, sir," Morecamb snapped.

"I do apologise," O' Toole replied without a shred of sincerity. "Anyway, we're all done here. Detective Inspector Morecamb will fill you in on the way home. Yes," he said as he walked away, "a very satisfactory outcome, I believe, for all concerned."

*****

Nagle drove, with McClean in the passenger seat while Morecamb sat in the back, in silence. With great difficulty he held back tears of rage. Nagle saw his struggles in the rear view mirror and motioned to McClean to stay quiet.

When he spotted the first pub with a decent parking lot Nagle pulled in, unclipped his seat belt and opened Morecamb's door.

"Let's grab ourselves a drink, Jim. You too, Al. What will ye have?"

"I'll have a double whiskey, on the rocks," Morecamb said.

"So will I," said McClean.

Two hours later Morecamb was still painfully sober. Nagle had restricted himself to two pints and McClean had kept pace with Morecamb and was now practically comatose. Nagle helped him into the back seat and put him lying across it. Morecamb now sat up front and the two men talked quietly for the rest of the journey.

Morecamb had told both men about the two interviews and what he termed O' Toole's treachery. At one stage Nagle had been afraid that Morecamb would give himself a heart attack. There was no consoling

him. He went on and on, about O'Toole, about the duplicitous nature of Lonergan and Wallace who, because of their machinations and lies, had walked straight into a trap which had been set by O' Toole and.........
who else? Drummond? Was he really the puppet master and, if he was, how could they prove it? How could they prove anything?

"Don't worry, Jim, we'll get him," Nagle said as he pulled out into the traffic. "He can't hide forever."

CHAPTER 48

It was nearly midnight when Nagle dropped Morecamb home. All the lights were off so he let himself in very quietly and, rather than disturb Jane, he decided he would sleep in the spare bedroom.

But sleep evaded him well into the night. In spite of his exhaustion the events of the day kept going around in his head. There were alternate feelings of self-loathing, anger and frustration with a fine dollop of self-pity thrown in. But, mostly, anger.

Eventually he fell into a fitful sleep though, if questioned, he would have declared that he didn't get a wink of sleep. But, he must have dozed off because he was awakened by Jane, shaking him and calling his name.

Abruptly he sat up in bed, desperately trying to get his bearings, conscious that he wasn't in his own bed but completely puzzled by his new surroundings.

"Jim, wake up," Jane whispered urgently. "There's someone at the door."

On tremulous legs he wobbled down the stairs blinking at the landing light which Jane had switched on.

"What time is it?" he mumbled.

"It's half past five in the morning," she answered indignantly. "Who, in God's name, would be calling on us at this hour of the morning?"

Gingerly, Morecamb opened the door and stared at the man standing in front of him.

"Jim!" Drummond's voice boomed in the stillness of the morning. "Looks like it was a rough one," he laughed as he took in Morecamb's dishevelled appearance. "And you must be the lovely Jane," Drummond said brushing past Morecamb and extending his hand in greeting.

"Yes", she said, her face creased in confusion.

"Jim, where are your manners? Never mind, I'm Pete Drummond, an old friend of Jim's. We go way back. I'm sorry for the unearthly hour but I need to run something by the boss."

"Oh, I see. Yes, it is an ungodly hour," she said. "Can I get you a tea or coffee?"

Then she noticed that Jim hadn't moved from the spot in front of the door and was looking at Drummond with scarcely concealed hatred.

"Or maybe not, Mr Drummond," Jane said quickly. "You'll excuse me. I'm going back to bed. I'll turn the light on in the kitchen. The sitting room is reserved for invited guests," and she turned on her heel and left the two men.

"Feisty, isn't she," laughed Drummond. "Nice little gaff you have here," he said conversationally. "Right, Morecamb, lead the way."

As if in a bad dream Morecamb walked ahead and plonked himself down on a chair. With bloodshot eyes he watched as Drummond brushed a few crumbs from another chair before sitting on it.

"Jim, you must be wondering _____."

"Why?" Morecamb snapped. "And let's cut to the chase. Let's have no bullshit."

Drummond had a slight smile on his lips and sat back, unbuttoning his overcoat with slow, deliberate movements.

"I thought you'd want to hear the good news, Jim."

"Good for whom? Yourself, no doubt."

"Well, no, I don't see how it could be of benefit to me. But you and your team will garner some brownie points. Lonergan and Wallace have confessed to the murder of Geoffrey Hunter."

Morecamb could hear the wind pick up outside. Somewhere in the distance a wicket gate creaked to and fro and a carpet of leaves suddenly cascaded against the kitchen window. The season was starting to turn, from summer to autumn, from bright colours to grey and soon 'the fall of the leaf' would be the new buzz word on everyone's lips, as if each had invented the phrase. And then the unrelenting emptiness of winter.

Drummond was smiling broadly at him now, very pleased with himself, like a conjurer who has just pulled the most amazing stunt. "And it will look good on your C.V., Jim, when you apply for the now vacant position of Superintendent and, who knows, in the fullness of time, even Commissioner. I've already put in a good word for you."

In spite of his rather delicate state Morecamb got up and walked over to the back door. He was afraid he was going to strike Drummond and wanted to put distance between them.

"But they didn't kill Hunter," Morecamb said flatly. It was a statement, not a question.

"Well, they confessed, Jim, and it seems to me _____."

"Shall I tell you what I think, Drummond?" said Morecamb and he came back and stood over his former friend. "Your pal, Cuthbert, killed Hunter, at your behest. I don't know why but I'll find out and when I do I'll take you down and O' Toole along with you."

"Proof, Jim. You know, that little, pesky component of all satisfactory convictions and you don't have any."

"I'll get proof. I'll throw every available resource at it and track down your assassin and, when I'm finished with him, he'll be singing like a canary."

"No, you won't," said Drummond pushing back his chair. "Cuthbert is a chameleon. I don't know how many aliases he has adopted down the years but you're deluding yourself if you think you'll be the one to capture him. He's a professional, one of the best," Drummond said quietly. "And, whilst I wouldn't exactly say he's loyal, nevertheless, I think we have a mutual respect for one another. And I pay very well."

"Everyone has a price, Drummond."

"Yes, there we agree," said Drummond as he started to button up his coat. "You have two men confessing to a murder on your patch and everybody will applaud that."

"And what's to stop them from retracting their statement?" Morecamb hissed. "A year or two incarcerated with every sort of low-life and _____."

"They won't. You said it yourself, everyone has a price. Well, Wallace has a disabled granddaughter who he adores. Securing the very best care for her doesn't come cheap and, of course, her safety is paramount. And then there's Lonergan who has his own little secret. He's hardly going to spend the last twenty years keeping it under wraps and suddenly decide to expose himself to public opprobrium."

"So," said Morecamb slowly, "good, old-fashioned blackmail."

"Oh, hardly that, Jim. It's such a nasty word. More a case of recognising the price of something they hold dear. After all, there must be something or someone that you feel protective about," he finished with a smirk.

Morecamb opened the back door and motioned to Drummond to get out. He didn't trust himself to speak.

"Oh, I nearly forgot, Jim. The enquiry into Sergeant Cassidy's death can be shelved and recorded as a simple hit and run. Happens all the time, don't you agree? And do you know something," he added in a voice full of menace, "your Jane reminds me so much of Sergeant Cassidy."

CHAPTER 49

Morecamb stood at the top of the Incident Room and looked around at his team. He didn't make eye contact with any of them. Idly he noticed that McClean seemed to be still intoxicated. He was glad to see Alderton among their number. Nagle had his eyes fixed on O' Toole who was standing beside Morecamb and who had felt 'duty bound' to be part of this 'special day'.

Suddenly Morecamb knew how a drowning man must feel, the sheer panic before the waters closed around him and blessed oblivion took over.

He decided to stick to the script and every word he uttered took him deeper into the flood waters.

"Superintendent Wallace and Inspector Lonergan have confessed to the murder of Superintendent Hunter," he began. "They will both be charged later today. I want to thank you all for your tireless work, for your dedication and, most importantly, your loyalty.

I also want to take a moment to remember Sergeant Gwen Cassidy and the dedication and zeal which she brought to this case. She will not be forgotten.

Her death will be consigned to the category of a 'hit and run'. Naturally we will keep the file open but, for the moment, our resources will be focussed elsewhere. Thank you all."

Nobody stirred or spoke. Morecamb picked up his folder and, as he headed towards the door, he heard O' Toole call for a round of applause for their 'dedicated and professional' detective inspector. Nobody applauded and as Morecamb reached the door the lone and incongruous clapping petered out and the silence reigned once more.

*****

Twenty four hours later Morecamb was standing at the top of Shandon Street. Below him lay the street lights of Cork city, reflecting on the rushing waters of the river Lee.

Somewhere in the distance he could hear the call of the corncrake, no doubt mustering his 'troops' in preparation for their long journey to warmer climes. The breeding season was now at an end. But they would be back. Would he still hear them singing in the Spring or had the sound of music died in that Incident Room a few short hours ago.

Somehow he had got through the day. He hadn't seen O' Toole again, McClean had gone AWOL and Alderton and Murphy had, unbidden, returned to the Cold Cases' unit. Nagle, in a written note, had tendered his resignation and left the station.

Now, Morecamb looked out across the city, at the intermittent lights of cars piercing the darkness and at the stars which seemed a million miles away and he knew that all the certainties in his life would never feel the same again.

The End

ABOUT THE AUTHOR

Susan is a retired teacher of English. Originally from Co. Cork she now lives in Limerick and is the mother of four grown-up children.

The success of her first novel 'Silent Lives' was a great impetus to complete and publish 'Betrayal', the second in the series of Inspector Morecamb stories. 'A Tangled Web' is the third book in the series. All three books are of the Crime fiction genre and are set in the late 60s in rural Ireland. She has had a number of topical articles published in 'Headstuff' and devotes most of her time to writing. She also enjoys gardening and walking.

PLEASE REVIEW

Dear Reader,

If you enjoyed this book, would you kindly post a short review about the book. Your feedback will make all the difference to getting the word out and help more readers find my book.

Thank you in advance

Susan

Printed in Great Britain
by Amazon

21804767R00128